CW00729458

that's write!

Eastern Counties
Edited by Allison Dowse

Disclaimer

Young Writers has maintained every effort
to publish stories that will not cause offence.

Any stories, events or activities relating to individuals
should be read as fictional pieces and not construed
as real-life character portrayal.

 Young**Writers**
First published in Great Britain in 2004 by:
Young Writers
Remus House
Coltsfoot Drive
Peterborough
PE2 9JX
Telephone: 01733 890066
Website: www.youngwriters.co.uk

All Rights Reserved

© Copyright Contributors 2004

SB ISBN 1 84460 518 3

Foreword

Young Writers was established in 1991 and has been passionately devoted to the promotion of reading and writing in children and young adults ever since. The quest continues today. *Young Writers* remains as committed to engendering the fostering of burgeoning poetic and literary talent as ever.

This year, *Young Writers* are happy to present a dynamic and entertaining new selection of the best creative writing from a talented and diverse cross section of some of the most accomplished secondary school writers around. Entrants were presented with four inspirational and challenging themes.

'Myths And Legends' gave pupils the opportunity to adapt long-established tales from mythology (whether Greek, Roman, Arthurian or more conventional eg The Loch Ness Monster) to their own style.

'A Day In The Life Of . . .' offered pupils the chance to depict twenty-four hours in the lives of literally anyone they could imagine. A hugely imaginative wealth of entries were received encompassing days in the lives of everyone from the top media celebrities to historical figures like Henry VIII or a typical soldier from the First World War.

Finally 'Short Stories', in contrast, offered no limit other than the author's own imagination while 'Hold The Front Page' provided the ideal opportunity to challenge the entrants' journalistic skills asking them to provide a newspaper or magazine article on any subject of their choice.

That's Write! Eastern Counties is ultimately a collection we feel sure you will love, featuring as it does the work of the best young authors writing today. We hope you enjoy the work included and will continue to return to *That's Write! Eastern Counties* time and time again in the years to come.

Contents

Earlham High School, Norwich
Thomas Mills (12)   32

Hardwick Middle School, Bury St Edmunds
Charlotte Wright (11)   33
Kelsey Butcher (12)   34

Hethersett High School, Norwich
Amber Curtis (14)   35

Kingsbrook School, Milton Keynes
Richard Smales (15)   36
Lara Sadler (12)   37
Abbie Stock (11)   38
Amy Sellman-Bartlett (13)   39
Tony Gallop (13)   40
Lauren Saunders (11)   41
Natasha Toms (11)   42
Kathryn Jenkins (12)   43
Scott Winkworth (12)   44
Rebecca Haigh (11)   45
Adam Lambert (13)   46
Emily Weissang (11)   47
Clare Booth (11)   48
Ben Keen-Toombs (11)   49
Daniel Welch (12)   50
Kayleigh Whitlock (12)   51
Thomas Basketfield (12)   52
Sarika Patel (12)   53
Felicia Gatenby (12)   54
Kieran Price (11)   55
Rebecca Houseago (11)   56
Matthew Leach (11)   57
Nicola Welch (12)   58
Sam White (12)   59
Zac White   60
Max Ikin (12)   61
Ashleigh Hall (12)   62
Emma Cumberlidge (11)   63
Matthew Krzywon (12)   64

Stephanie Drew (13)   98
Daniel Ritchie (12)   99

Oak Bank School, Leighton Buzzard
Joshua Campbell (14)   100

St Bernard's RC High School for Girls, Westcliff-on-Sea
Lee-Anne Pawley (14)   101
Rosie Underhill (13)   102
Alice Nutman (12)   103
Emma Marie Lynch (12)   104
Chantelle Ryan (13)   105
Rhiannon Thomas (13)   106
Shelby Ryan (13)   107
Marie Goldsworthy (13)   108
Sophie Lark (13)   109
Sarah Rimmington (12)   110
Michelle Regnaud-Carvalho (11)   111
Rebecca Miller (12)   112
Jessica Ackland (12)   113
Jade-Louise Fort (12)   114
Georgia Chapelle (12)   115
Melissa Bonnelame (12)   116
Emma Sampford (12)   117
Robyn Strauss (11)   118
Catherine Birch (12)   119
Tiffany Bryan (11)   120
Rachel Gibson (13)   121
Priscilla Kananji (13)   122
Leanne Elcoate (12)   123

St John Fisher RC School, Peterborough
Shamreen Bi (13)   124
Sam Harwin (13)   125
Ethan Nash (13)   126
Leah Hobbs (14)   127
Becky Weston (13)   128
Hannah Hill (13)   130
Matthew Phillips (14)   131
Josephine Caulkett (13)   132

Swavesey Village College, Swavesey

The Beaconsfield School, Beaconsfield

The Parkside School (MLD), Norwich

The Perse School, Cambridge

The Creative Writing

A Day In The Life Of A Puppy

(For Scamper who has just had a litter and for Izzy who's just had one too!)

I want to tell you about the time when my eyes opened. I was only seventeen days old so forgive me if the details are a little foggy . . .

I was refreshing myself with some milk when mother growled, 'Not so hard, you little hellhound.' I was in the mood for a grizzle. I asked Mother to wash my eyes as they were sore. 'Is it time?' she muttered to herself whilst she washed. Her tongue was so soothing that I didn't bother answering.

I was jolted awake from my doze as a searing pain coursed through me. As I screamed, the pain began to subside and a thousand colours swam into view. A human picked me up and I stopped. Humans are so ugly. I turned to see Mother but Mother wasn't there. A huge beast with large teeth and shaggy fur gaped at me. I sank my gums into the human's claw and it tried to feed me to the beast. I started scrambling away but the beast's teeth clamped round my ribs and as it picked me up I knew that everything would be OK. It was Mother, the mother that smelt of meat and as she put me down I began to sway. I hadn't expected Mother to look like this. I needed milk but as I staggered towards her side I just wanted to sleep and all at once I was dreaming, dreaming of colours, of Mother, of humans, of meat, of, of . . .

Lauren Atherall (13)
Archbishop Sancroft High School, Harleston

A Day In The Life Of My Smelly Old English Book

It smelt nicer than ever this morning, those mouldy sandwiches are really taking effect. Shuffled about a bit, then that big maths book pushed me, telling me to go back to sleep. Just because he has a lot of complicated things in his pages doesn't mean he owns the bag.

Drifted in and out of sleep, thought about my troubled childhood. How I never knew my parents, just this dark bag and the occasional mouldy sandwich. Got teased by a pencil case about having no name. It's not that I object to being an exercise book, it's just my name could be either 'Samuel Richards', 'English' or 'Mrs Watkins'. If only I had one name, life would be so much easier

Got taken out with that new book. Doesn't talk much. Probably because his name is so long it could be 'The' or 'Fellowship' or 'Of' or 'Ring'. Strange, he don't half weigh loads. Glad to get back to my nice dark bag. The dictionary says I am agoraphobic. I said, 'Trust you to know all the big words!'

Samuel Richards (13)
Archbishop Sancroft High School, Harleston

A Day In The Life Of A Penny

I fell out of Tom's pocket today, when he pulled out his handkerchief. I lay there, winking in the sun for a bit, then a small child came up and put me in his mouth. Yuck! It smelt like bananas. Then his mum came up and said, 'Rodney what have you got there? Argh! Take it out!' She wrenched me out of his mouth and put me in a purse. Had a good chat with a 10p. He was brand new, all shiny.

Suddenly there was a gleam of light and the purse opened. I was taken out with a pound and 20p.

A lady said, 'That should be enough for dinner.'

We were grabbed by a dirty, sweaty hand and shoved into a pocket. But the pocket had a hole in and we fell right through it, down the trouser leg and into a drain. Wheeeee! Ah, rest at last.

Ella Chubbock (13)
Archbishop Sancroft High School, Harleston

A Day In The Life Of Timothy Thompson

Why did Mum and Dad have to split up? Why did we have to move to a new house, in a new town? Doesn't anybody care about me? I've got enough problems already.

Mum should try being an unpopular, 12-year-old boy with learning difficulties, and his voice breaking every 5 minutes. Except Mum wouldn't notice if my bum was on fire with Kate around. Honestly, she's 2 years old and she's being treated like a part of the Royal Family. What's so great about a drooling toddler? Mark my words, one day I'm going to go insane.

First day of school today. Great, I'm sat next to a fat girl called Candice who is like a big marshmallow. She has her hair up in two bunches and she looks like she has just spilt flour all over her face. One almost-friend. No. She will give me a bad start to my new reputation. Oh well, it will go well with my awful teacher, Mrs Briggs.

'Come and introduce yourself to your new class,' she squeaked, obviously trying to pull a false smile.

'Um, hi!' I spluttered, trying to sound cool and relaxed. 'I'm Timothy Thompson.'

The whole class laughed, even Mrs Briggs smirked.

'Carry on, dear.'

'I've just moved into Mulldgusry.' As I said this my voice broke. I knew my first day of school would go badly.

Eleanor Sieveking (12)
Archbishop Sancroft High School, Harleston

A Day In The Life Of A Tortoise

As my eyes grew accustomed to the ever increasing light, I realised where I was, why I was there and what was happening to me. But one thought kept creeping into my buzzing head, *Catherine, was she alright? Was she still alive?*

My movements were slow and monotonous but I gradually turned my head and focused my onyx eyes on the dark shape next to me. My heart leapt, there she was - Catherine, my soulmate.

Suddenly my body clock clicked and started ticking, sending a jolt through it like a bolt of lightning. Automatically my legs started moving in time with my beating heart. This was alright, but was Catherine? Again I twisted my head round, it was such an effort to move, such a laborious task, but she seemed good enough; my mind was now almost at peace and so my attentions turned to my surroundings.

I looked forwards towards the vast expanse of sand, and lying across the horizon was the gateway into the other world. The world of noise, bright lights and fast movements. At this point food dropped down from above delivering our harvest. My head drew back into my shell but I faced forward again. I had to eat. I moved, so did Catherine. I walked, so did she, I ran as fast as I could - she did too. Then we were out in the open, in front of us lay a beautiful carpet of dandelions. There it began, life after hibernation.

Jennifer Roberts (14)
Archbishop Sancroft High School, Harleston

A Day In The Life Of A Raindrop

Hi! I'm Gleam, don't really know why though because I'm dull and see-through. Mum said she called me that because she thought that she'd never have a baby, and then I came and was a glimmer of hope! Really soppy I know but that's how mums are. Haven't seen her for a while mind you, I think she fell somewhere, I hope it was in the sea. It's every raindrop's ambition to fall in the sea. I've only dropped once in my little life. I fell in the Amazon, and you'll never guess what happened to me? I was sucked up by an elephant! It was really weird going through all the tubes and then I shot out through the other end! It was so cool! I just sat there with some friends I met along the way and it started to get really hot. Suddenly I flew up, up and up into a cloud. That's where I am now, and it's a bit cramped in here.

Hang on a minute - something's happening! Ooh! Drops are starting to fall, wow! Whooosshhh! Oh, ow, ee! Hmmph, a roof. Oh well - maybe the sea next time!

Abby Thomas (12)
Archbishop Sancroft High School, Harleston

Africa's Call

'Listen to me child.'

'I'm listening.' Looking into the deep pools of his eyes, I could only see a flicker of the light that used to shine there. The torch had gone out a long time ago.

'Promise me you will remember her.' His voice was now nothing above a rusty groan.

'I will remember, Grandpa. For both of us.'

I felt a light pressure on my hand and watched his face change. It was so subtle a change that a stranger might not have noticed. But I was no stranger. Where there had once been unrest was now only contentment. Finally there was peace. His spirit had been released from the cage it had been imprisoned in ever since he was a boy.

I staggered out of the darkness and into the early dawn. The close air of the hut had been cutting away at my very soul. Tears stained my vision. But I was not sad that Grandpa had gone. I was sad that I could not follow.

I willed myself not to forget. Grandpa, one day I shall follow you. I know that you will be waiting. Waiting in Africa's open arms.

Jennifer Clay (14)
Archbishop Sancroft High School, Harleston

Ragnarok

In the eternal hellfire of Tartarus, Coronus Titan of time was beginning to get excited. After thousands of millennia, Zeus and the other accursed gods had grown weak. All that was needed was the final step.

Claire Radcliff was fully ready for her expedition. 'After all,' she reasoned, 'if this comes off I'll be more famous than Indiana Jones!'

Claire's good mood continued as she stepped out of the whirling 'copter onto the tiny island of Imonus. Her bright spirit slackened slightly as she progressed through the sunless jungle but still she pressed on, her natural fighting spirit forcing her to the centre of Imonus. Then she stopped.

The twin statues beside the door depicted a handsome long-haired man with sword drawn wearing full battle armour. But this was not what had caught Claire's attention. It was the air, the very feeling of the place - like *time* itself was imprisoned. However, still Claire ventured on. Rushing past the statues, she flung open the doors . . . and rebounded, her frail form swelling with mystic energies, warping her body beyond any recognition.

The island was enveloped in a thick blanket of purest darkness. The foolish girl had shattered the barrier the gods created long ago. Now Coronus and the Titans walked the Earth once again. The ravens gathered once more round Valagard Plain. The gods themselves descended to war.

Ragnarok begins.

Paul Karoubas (12)
Archbishop Sancroft High School, Harleston

A Day In The Life Of A Daisy

I open my golden yellow petals. The ground that I am planted in is infested with wildlife, it is like a jungle. *Crunch, crunch* go the ants as they carry dead, brittle leaves past me. Before I know it I have a black and yellow bee land on my sweet-smelling petals going to collect pollen.

There I was lapping up the sun's golden rays. I could feel the vibrations coming closer and closer. I could see their pink and yellow summer dresses and their very flip, floppy sandals. It was four little girls. They sat down on a brown, fat, stumpy bench. One by one Bod, Fred, Andy and Jo were gone like a flash. Their dying words were 'Help!' Then, thank God, they were gone. All was quiet.

Stomp! One came back like thunder and stomped on me. My life was over.

Paul Berry (16)
Bungay High School, Bungay

A Day In The Life Of A Tropical Fish

I feel the morning, warm all around me. The golden sequins of sunshine swimming the water. I shake my multicoloured tail and begin to move gently, gliding like a piece of seaweed in the water. I see the bottom of the ocean, sandy and golden. A shoal of blue neons swim past me like a burst of thunder, then disappear.

My sight is almost gone. I swim fast, and get faster. My sight is back. A glisten touches my eye gently like a leaf falling to the ground. I swim towards it because it looks interesting. Almost close. *Snap.* Nothing left but a stone-like creature which is actually a clam. I toss around in the water, as the force from the clam was like a whirlwind. Lose interest. I swim away.

Two fish playing in the aqua atmosphere. Peek-a-boo. Go and join them. I get rejected by the fish as they carry on. I feel upset. I glide to the nearest rock and hide behind it. Stay there for a while feeling sorry for myself, in the dark, deserted hole.

Forgot why I was there. Glide out quickly to find something to do. Behind me I feel the water moving and begin to get scared. Rush back to the stone taking quick breaths. Almost there. Rush faster. I see black.

Now I see nothing, feel nothing and do nothing. Don't even move a muscle.

Abbi Ling (15)
Bungay High School, Bungay

A Day In The Life Of An Ant

Thud! Thud! I looked out to see what was going on, there were children running around, some were sitting there having a nice little picnic. I could smell something, it was a sweet smell, it smelt a bit like strawberries. As I marched on the smell was stronger and stronger. I crawled out of my colony, I stepped into something really sticky, it was that gorgeous smell, it tasted really nice. I wanted to get it back into my colony to share with my family and friends.

I didn't want to go home to ask for help to bring it in, I was afraid someone else would snatch it. So I tried to drag it, it wouldn't budge my feet were really sticky now. The strawberry sticky stuff was attached to a stick. I tried to pull it by the stick, it still wouldn't budge.

Thud! Thud! A black shadow appeared over me, I dived out of the way. That was a close one! I almost got trodden on . . . where was the gorgeous sticky stuff? I couldn't smell it, I spent a long time looking for it but then I got tired so I went back home.

There it was, right in front of me, the child had kicked it in the direction of my home. I felt ecstatic and ran towards it like lightning. I dived into it - *bad idea*. I was struggling, panicking, I couldn't get out, it was so sticky. I realised I didn't really like this sweet.

Craig Jones (15)
Bungay High School, Bungay

A Day In The Life Of A Soldier

I woke up to the sound of the reveille. I could smell the sweat of all the soldiers in my barrack. It was 4am, I looked out of my window. I could see it was going to be a long cold day, as the mist was beginning to cover the hills.

I quickly put on my uniform, because the sarge was knocking on the heavy, wooden, solid door. As he entered everyone stood to attention shivering in their boots. He appeared big, bold and bad, someone you would *not* argue with. The instructions he gave were short and precise.

'Right you lot get ready for a run, I think a mile is enough before breakfast.'

The moors were cold and damp following the morning dew which made the tracks more slippery. It was difficult to keep my balance.

Shane Brabbin (16)
Bungay High School, Bungay

A Day In The Life Of A Peasant

Bang! A brick hit the tall dark wall beside me as loud as a drum. My breakfast stank of effluence. I could hear the boss shouting my name. I can't wash, I feel so dirty, my hands are blackened with dirt.

I finished my eggy water and slice of stale brown bread breakfast as quickly as possible. I have black and blue bruises on my back, my boss beats me if I'm late.

The pigs are my first stop. This morning on the farm was the last for five pigs. I had to kill them for my boss's tea tonight. I took them to the chamber of death, pig goes in, chops come out. First the head comes off, with one flick of a machete. The red blood spurting from its neck.

My lunch however had such a sickening look and smell, it was not worth eating. It came up 10 minutes after eating it. After the pigs it was horses, then the cows.

The big black and brown cows were looking into my eyes. The terror in their faces was terrible, like a shark was about to attack them.

I went home to my barn of wood, the walls riddled with holes. When it rains everything gets wet. There's puddles of muddy and gritty water. Just a straw floor is my house. My big bed of soggy wet straw.

I took off my brown cloth underwear, mud-stained. I went to bed, to dream of a better world, where everyone is equal and the grass is green.

Andrew Symonds (16)
Bungay High School, Bungay

A Day In The Life Of My Brother!

I wake up at 6am to eat my fresh slugs and slime. I take a dip in the pond for my morning wash, *splash!*

It's time to begin my reign of terror at school. I start by eating dirt then I flick bogies at teachers.

It's time for lunch, chips, pizza and my favourite drink, Coke.

I return home at 3.40pm, this is the best bit of the day, wind my sisters up, run, run, run weaving in and out of my sisters as they chase me. Winding up my sisters is great, what really winds them up is shouting and singing loudly with my squeaky voice. It sounds like a nail scraping down a blackboard then I hit them and run away. I get all of them ganging up on me like a bull running towards a red cloth. The best bit though is winding them up, then they get wrong so I escape.

After all the fun I've had in my day I take a walk with my mates and play ding, dong, dash!

It's bedtime now but I don't go to bed yet I go when I like because I'm a *brat* as my sisters would say!

Martina Jackson (15)
Bungay High School, Bungay

UFO Spotting

Yesterday, on 31st March 04, a suspected UFO flew over the Earth. Police reports tell us that this is true and there might be a possible 'landing'.

Do you believe in UFOs? Mr King certainly does. Here is his description.

'It was 11.39pm when the UFO flew over our house. It made a very loud noise like somebody playing on a keyboard. I rushed out of the house to see what was going on but all I could see was green, blue, red and yellow flashing all over the place. They were so bright that it nearly blinded me. Suddenly, the light dimmed and there it was - a humungous UFO hovering above me. I did not stop to double-check, I just ran for my life back to the house. Once I was in, I locked all the doors and all the windows. I was safe.

That was the most frightening experience in my whole life and I hope it doesn't happen again'.

The same UFO was spotted at 12.04am by Mr Sanders in Ukraine. He told us the exact same story but he also told us that he was sure he saw a form of beast or creature inside it.

Police may also have caught the UFO on a speed camera. This tells us the speed the UFO was travelling at.

Scientists are becoming frantic after they discovered there may be a 'landing' and are frightened about them taking over Earth. The final question is . . . is there intelligent life out there?

Emily Smart (13)
Chantry High School, Ipswich

A Day In The Life Of A White Tiger

Sasha closed her eyes and heard the rushing sound of clear water. She opened them and saw a beautiful lush green forest, laden with tropical fruit, and home to the white tiger. Not many, though. Over many years, Sasha had witnessed her family dying out. Watched them fade as they got wiped out.

The breeze blowing in Sasha's face called out to her, a message from her ancestors. Sasha's life was riddled with mystery. She had seen the feared hunter before on many occasions. They were fast, intelligent and deadly.

Sasha streaked out from under a towering tree, and her two cubs, Sugar and Snowball, came scrambling out after her. Deer. Food. But as she drew nearer - *bang!* Sasha skidded to a halt. She could smell burning from a gun. Hunters were here.

She darted back to her cubs, picked them up and flung them hurriedly onto her back, and fled for their lives. They were going somewhere hunters had never been before.

She flashed through the forest with her cubs tumbling over each other on her broad, stripy back. As she sprinted through the trees, the surrounding environment got darker and rougher. Overgrown thistles tugged at Sasha's white fur. As day faded around them, the cubs squeaked in terror.

There! A cave stood there, towering over the white tigers. Sasha purred at the gently dripping rock. The hunters would never find her here.

Stephanie Moussa (12)
Chantry High School, Ipswich

A Day In The Life Of Kim Jansson, Speedway Rider

It's 1am and I'm sitting on the plane to England. I rode last night for my Swedish club, Kaparna, where I top scored. Tonight I'm riding for my English club, Ipswich, at a place called Arena Essex. I enjoy riding for Ipswich a lot, and I think they like me riding for them. Tonight, I'm staying at a hotel near Foxhall Stadium, which is very handy.

I'm now landing at Stansted Airport. I know this place like the back of my hand, as I'm backwards and forwards to Sweden and England. At least I don't have to go to Poland!

I've got my bags now. I've only got my kit bag and a tiny bag with spare clothes in. I'm waiting to be picked up by my mechanic. There he is. He'll take me to Ipswich to get ready and load up.

It's now 5pm, and I'm at Arena Essex in the pits. I'm sorting the bikes out for tonight. It's getting on now, so I'm going to get changed.

It's 7.30 now. I can see the Ipswich fans, some of them follow us everywhere! They're now introducing me, I'd better wave. Good, it's time for the first race. We win 5-1. Now I'm out for my first ride. I hope I do well.

It's the end of the meeting here. We won 49-41, with me scoring 10 + 2 points. This, I am very proud of. I'm going to get changed now whilst my mechanics pack away. I can't believe I scored so much tonight. It must be my best match yet.

Amy Carpenter (13)
Chantry High School, Ipswich

A Day In The Life Of An American Soldier In Iraq

We were awoken by loud shouting and screaming, then there was gunfire and bangs which sounded like small bombs, there was more gunfire and then it all went quiet again.

We got into uniform and put on our helmets and got our guns from the storage units. We went outside. We were being fired at immediately. It was a big rotten trap. The gunfight lasted for about an hour, but seemed to last forever.

There were people laying dead everywhere, hundreds of Iraqi civilians laying around dead all over the place. We don't know who attacked us but we think it was Iraqi rebels. Nineteen soldiers have been killed so far this week. Gunfire seems to go off every 10 minutes.

Because of all the gunfire we haven't eaten properly or slept properly for four days and when we're not fighting we're clearing up dead people.

I just want to curl up in a ball and watch everything go away. Please just let everything go away - please.

Michael Brooks (13)
Chantry High School, Ipswich

A Day In The Life Of A World War I Soldier

Here I am, sitting in filth, mud and germs. Rats scurrying around me and soldiers dropping dead from illness. Bombs descending towards me that shake me from my sleep. Day dawns and I'm already positioned in my muddy trench and gunning down Germans. I skip breakfast and I'm almost fainting with hunger when a bowl of liquid is put down in front of me. I devour it. When I peep over the trench, there are nearly 50 dead bodies in no-man's-land, and there are more every day. Someone's father, son, cousin, nephew or uncle.

Every day there are 10, maybe 15 dead bodies carted out of the trenches. Every night 5 bombs fall, 10 die every day and I'm not one of them. Every time I wish I was dead, someone else dies. And there is nothing I can do about it. Every day an epidemic comes round, I desperately try to catch it. But I don't. I'm obviously destined to fight this war to the end. But I want to die. I shout, 'God, please let me die.'

Bombs fall and I cry myself to sleep. I dream the war is over. But it's just the beginning. Over and over in my head a voice shouts, 'It's just the beginning.'

Amy Witham (12)
Chantry High School, Ipswich

Deadly Jungle

Deep in the Amazon Jungle, Professor Boff, Mad Jack and a girl called Rebecca who was an orphan in Egypt had made a life in the jungle after their plane crashed on the way to an archaeology excavation. Mad Jack could speak to animals, Professor Boff was a brainiac and Rebecca could cook. They had found a friend called Tantore who was an elephant and a gorilla called Turk.

One day Rebecca found lots of dead fish in the nearby water supply, so she ran back and took the other two there, but then a tribe called Manjis captured them and accused them of poisoning their water and making their people sick. They were taken to the Manji camp where they were locked up. About fifteen minutes later Mad Jack was let out, and the Manji leader said, 'People dressed like you came and poisoned water.'

The leader said that if he didn't get rid of the problem he'd kill the other two.

Mad Jack and the strongest tribal man headed up the mountain towards the smoke, only to find gold diggers. The fumes and waste from their machines was going into the water thus poisoning it, so they fought a gang of men with guns then tied them up. They broke all their machinery and destroyed everything.

When they got back the other two were released and within days the water was safe again.

Aaron Scott (13)
Chantry High School, Ipswich

UFO?

Last night, a strange phenomenon was seen 'flying' through the skies of Britain.

Sightings of the object were recorded in Edinburgh, London, Manchester, Liverpool and Birmingham. Many people saw bright lights hovering no more than 400ft above the ground, followed by a great flash of electric-blue before disappearing. Witnesses gazed in wonder at the starry night as it hung there for at least five minutes. Some grabbed their video cameras to gather evidence

One witness said, 'I don't know what it was; there was just this huge flashing thing in the sky'.

The incident happened between the hours of 9pm and 12pm. Some claim it was a UFO they saw! The amazing floating object excited scientists, who say that it is absolutely incredible. However, lots disagree with this theory and say there is a rational explanation such as a military experiment

By this morning, there was no trace of the 'craft' which set the nation's minds working. It seems as though we may never find an explanation to the lights we saw last night in the sky, but we can hope that one day we will know if there truly is, something out there.

Chelsie Cattermole (13)
Chantry High School, Ipswich

The UFET

Yesterday, under the cover of darkness, an alien spaceship came down from the sky and landed on the roof of Chantry High School and abducted all of the English teachers for being too strict with pupils, by giving them detentions for no apparent reason, which is just evil.

One of the pupils who was given detention a lot was Axel Shovel, his teacher gave him detention for doing his homework, along with quite a few others.

All of the pupils jumped for joy when those evil creatures were taken away hopefully forever! I talked to some of the pupils who were in class at the time of the abduction. Fester Cornflake told me that aliens came through the door and the teacher ran to close the door but she got sucked into a gigantic hover-type thing.

I also talked to Owan Alive, he said he was jumping around when his wretched teacher got sucked up.

All of the pupils are having parties to celebrate the disappearance of the teachers!

Lester Blake (13)
Chantry High School, Ipswich

Terrorist Attack

Yesterday on the 31st March there was a terrorist attack at Felixstowe docks. The time was 7.46pm and lasted for two minutes. There were 62 people killed and 236 injured.

Two bombs were set, each either side of the docks. However the docks were not largely damaged. In fact there was more damage to the workers. Most people who worked there and visitors were dead before the rescue services were there.

Pictures were taken by a security camera set high above the docks, but the camera did not get any film or pictures of the attackers.

Here is a quote from an eye witness from the scene.

'The attack was very quick but there were two very big bombs on the east and west sides of the docks. I didn't see any of the attackers, only workers being killed by the bombs'.

Thomas Winkworth (13)
Chantry High School, Ipswich

The Blood On The Bedroom Wall

Kate stood outside the front door waiting for her dad to get the keys. When she walked in she felt a chill run down her spine!

'You know it's late,' said her dad, 'you should get some sleep.'

The next day Kate started redecorating her bedroom. She pulled her bed away from the wall so she could pull off the old wallpaper. 'Argh!' There on the wall was a giant bloodstain. Kate didn't want to worry her dad so she didn't say anything about it.

That night Kate was in the bathroom getting ready for bed. As she was putting her toothbrush away she heard a voice from down the plughole. 'Who's that?' asked Kate.

'My name is Mary Baker. I was trapped down here after I moved into this house,' said the voice.

'Why are you down there?' said Kate.

'Oh no, he's coming!' said the voice.

There was a silence.

'Ha, ha, ha you'll never get out of here alive Kate,' said a creepy voice.

Kate started screaming and ran to her dad's room, but when she ran in he wasn't there! She looked out of the window, there was her dad hanging from a tree, the rope tightly round his neck and only one hand. Kate picked up a smashed bottle and walked around the room. A hand suddenly shot out from under the bed. Kate quickly sliced the arm off, then there was a flash and there was her dad smiling at her . . .

Kaysha Studd (12)
Chantry High School, Ipswich

Cancer Crisis!

This is ridiculous! I mean my own dad has gone to the doctors; and no one will tell me why! I'll bet even Carl knows. But do I? No.

Carl's my stupid big brother. He's four years older than me and thinks he knows everything. He doesn't though, I mean even Albert Einstein didn't know everything.

'Mel, come here and give me a hand with this table, your gran's tired out!' Mum's just shouted.

'OK, be there in a couple of secs!' I shout back. I walk in to find Gran sitting there huffing and puffing, moaning and groaning.

'It's stupid, getting a woman of my age to lift bloomin' tables about!' she mumbles to herself.

I go over to my mum and ask her why she wants to move the table.

'To keep my mind off your dad!' she bursts out. She then breaks down in tears.

'Mum? What's the matter? Why do you want to take your mind off Dad for? What's wrong with him?' I ask anxiously.

'Mel, go to your room, love,' says Gran, walking over to Mum, who is sitting on the sofa. 'Now, please!'

I run out of the room, crying. I stand near the door and listen.

'Now, Sharron, you can't carry on like this. You have to stay strong, if not for you, for the kids. You don't even know yet if he's actually got cancer.'

Cancer? Dad? *No!*

Sophie Gibson (12)
Chantry High School, Ipswich

Forest Camp

Katie, Sarah and Kevin were all sitting on the minibus chattering away. They were travelling to Forest Camp on a school trip. They had all been on the minibus for a considerable amount of time and they were starting to get tired. Time soon passed and before they knew it they were there. The scenery was beautiful; lakes glistening in the sunlight and tall pine trees blowing.

When they awoke the sun had already set. Today the whole group were going canoeing down Forest Camp's lake. Everyone was excited because it was the first time for everyone. An instructor was due at 10am for a safety talk before entering the deep waters.

'I can't wait!' shouted Sarah.

'Ssshhh - here he comes.'

Katie, Kevin and Sarah all shared a canoe and set off down river.

'Stop!' shouted Kevin. 'What the heck was that?'

'What?' replied Sarah.

'I . . . just saw . . . well a woman kind of thing floating on the river,' replied Kevin shakily.

'Grab the oar or we're gonna drop it,' shouted Katie. Katie held out her arm in a desperate struggle to reach it, only to fall in headfirst!

Katie was not a confident swimmer. Out of nowhere she felt a force pushing her.

'Grab her!' shouted Kevin.

Katie reached the boat safely. 'What happened?'

Later on that evening they all discovered that a young lady drowned in the river who went by the name of Helen. She is a spirit and saves anyone from drowning because she did. Katie was lucky and might not be alive if it wasn't for Helen.

Fern Simpson (13)
Chantry High School, Ipswich

Untitled

The crowd was electric, Michael had won the toss and elected to bat. He and Marcus opened and raced to 10 off the first over. Z Khan, the Indian opening bowler, had a confident LBW appeal which was given out by umpire Billy Bowden. I came in, in the second over I smashed my first ball for 4.

10 overs had gone, we were 107-1. Then we fell to pieces.

After 40 overs we were 210-7.

In the last 10 overs me and Simon put on a partnership of 120 and we finished on 330-7. After our 50 overs I had 107.

India started their innings needing 331 to win. They opened with Verinder Sehwag and the little master Sachin Tendulkar.

After 10 overs they were in full control Sehwag was on 60 and Sachin was on 73 so they were 133-0. I came into the attack and struck the first blow.

My first ball pitched one leg stump and swung back in and bowled him. After 20 they were 240-1. The next 25 were ours, they got 60 for 5 wickets. They needed 35 with 4 wickets in hand.

It was the last over, I bowled it. They needed 4 to win. My first ball was a dot. 2nd and 3rd dot, 4th and 5th singles. They needed 2 off the last ball. I bowled a Yorker, it rattled the batsman's pads - it was out.

We'd won the World Cup. It was great.

Grant Salisbury (13)
Chantry High School, Ipswich

The Rich Niece

London, a typical morning in March, the rain splattering the skin of unfortunate passers-by, the wind curling its long crooked fingers around them, the dim oil lamps burning dry in their holders, with fog clouding the eyes of those who walk by. But something is out of place, a girl dangling her legs over the dock wall. She has golden curls twisted tightly into a bun, her maroon dress fluttering in the breeze, two shiny black shoes buckled neatly to her feet, and a feathered hat perched on her head. A carriage pulls up to the kerb, which she instantly takes. As she looks out of the window her gaze is met. In one of the shop doors a homeless man glares back at her with longing. At last she reaches her destination. Her uncle, chest puffed out, greets her himself!

The carriage passes through the cold iron gates. In the foyer a young maid with a grim expression on her face, leads her to a room with a four-poster bed and a portrait of her uncle dominating the candlelit room. Faded tapestries are draped on the walls.

She unpacks her bags and sits in her nightgown upon her bed. She smiles - *perhaps this isn't going to be so bad*, she thinks. The maid enters with a small supper before bed and briskly takes out the dirty travelling clothes. She eats cheerfully, then the maid puts out the dim candles. Barely awake, the girl looks to the painting. Her eyes widen, she runs out screaming. The painting's empty, that's why she's screaming . . .

Megan Johnson (12)
Chantry High School, Ipswich

Woodcraft Folk Invade Lockerbrook

May 2003

Lockerbrook Here We Come

The minibus left Tesco's at 7.30am loaded down with rucksacks and walking boots. After lunch at Cumber Park we arrived at Lockerbook in the Peak District in time for tea.

Lockerbrook is a large house on the side of a hill surrounded by trees and fields, used as a youth hostel. We had a huge bedroom full of bunk beds.

After dinner we went on a night walk to explore the area.

Day Two

A very exciting day - we went up the climbing wall and took part in team challenges. After lunch we went caving and got soaked in the waterfall. After tea there was Morris dancing and music and singing.

Day Three

We climbed Kinder Scout and had lunch at the summit. We were supposed to be following a compass to a statue on the mountain but ended up in a ditch and got covered in mud from head to toe. We really needed a shower when we got back.

Day Four

Today we went rock hopping, we managed to get through all the gaps. Everything was great until my leader pushed me in the water and I got soaking wet but we got him back.

After lunch we put on helmets and harnesses and went abseiling over an 80ft bridge. *Very scary!*

Time To Go Home

Day five - After cleaning up we got in the minibus and said goodbye to Lockerbrook and our exciting adventure holiday.

Chloe Elmer (11)
Chantry High School, Ipswich

The Painting

He swept the brush roughly across the canvas and stood back to survey his work. It was an odd painting but the best he had done for a long time. The best *he* had done. By anyone else's standard it would be considered meaningless - a painting with no depth. However, Christoff was proud of his work. He had been depressed for a long time but this gave him hope, Christoff felt a strange sense of completion.

A shrill voice rushed down the stone stairway into the draughty cellar where Christoff was working. His spirits dropped in an instant and he slowly shuffled around to hear what his wife had to say.

'Hurry up, dinner's ready,' Christoff's cursed wife shrieked.

As he swung round, Christoff's elbow caught the edge of a small tub of bleach. The tub fell and splatters of bleach seeped into Christoff's painting. With a shout he reached for a rag and gently tried to soak up the bleach. He couldn't give up on his painting now.

'Christoooooff,' shrieked his wife impatiently.

Christoff dropped the bleachy rag into his metal sink and stomped up the stairs.

After a measly dinner of nothing much Christoff rushed down the cellar stairs to see if his painting was ruined. He stared at it. The bleach stains had nearly vanished, leaving pale marks where they had been. Christoff began to see shapes in the faint stains. The stains added something to the painting that made it unique. Christoff smiled triumphantly.

Bethan Jones (12)
City of Norwich School, Norwich

The Bridge

He looked through a hole in the wood. All he could see was cliff and shadow. There were some cracks in the cliff face which had plants sprouting out.

He wanted to jump, he really did, but it was an awfully long way down if he didn't make it. He felt ill just looking down.

He looked up. Some birds flew over the chasm; when they squawked it echoed around the rocky sides of the gorge and did not stop for ages as though there was no end to the hole and it had no bottom. He swallowed hard and put his foot down on the remaining wood of the bridge. It fell away.

He jumped back on his remaining foot. He could hear the shouted threats of the other boys, still lost in the woods behind him.

A slab of stone was left, beneath where the wood had fallen away. He stepped lightly onto it. It felt reasonably safe and he started to walk.

Then he heard the faint thud of the boys' footsteps behind him on the pathway. He turned around and saw them in the distance; he had to run for it.

As he started to run, part of the wood underneath fell away under the weight of him. He had to jump or he'd fall with the bridge.

He leapt, hoping he would make it. He landed hard on the dry, yellow grass.

Crash! The bridge fell behind him.

Michael Jennings (12)
City of Norwich School, Norwich

Holiday From Hell

A team of schoolchildren from Eaton High School were shocked when they arrived at their destination at Chateau Beaumont, Normandy, to find a dump.

We had an undercover journalist there, Thomas Mills, who was shocked as well.

The food was rubber, especially the frogs' legs and chicken. He starved himself for three days because of the terrible food. Then he went to the entertainment. That was okay but not brilliant. Eventually he thought he would have a comfy night but how he was wrong! The beds moved by themselves, the ceiling had lots of holes in it and the showers only let out cold water.

In the morning he went to the activities. He thought they were brilliant.

During the week he went to two castles. They were okay he thought and because he is a chocoholic he bought lots of chocolate. On the last day he went to Disneyland Resort, Paris and everyone was happy to get home.

Now we have some quotations from the school and the chateau: Miss Panning said, 'We will certainly not be going again'.

The Head said, 'I am disgusted with the chateau'.

The chateau staff said, 'We live up to the standards expected by the Normandy Council'.

The owner said, 'No comment'.

After this matter the school have decided not to go there again.

Thomas Mills (12)
Earlham High School, Norwich

The Meeting

I remember it as if it was yesterday. It was late, too late and too late for a child of my age, nine, to be out. So late that I did something that I would regret and would change my life forever. I went through the woods.

So I started walking, it was fine at first, but then I heard some branches snap so I quickened my pace, wrapping my scarf tighter around me. I felt the trees, dark and black were closing in on me.

I looked at my watch, it was half-past eight, and the moon was full and the night sky full of stars. Not that I could see it through the black mass of trees.

Suddenly some leaves went crunch, the rustling echoing in my ears, I turned around to look behind me and there stood a man towering over me like a giant. He had dark brown eyes, cruel and evil and he looked as if he hadn't shaved for weeks. He was wearing a green coat, tattered and torn. He wore dirty blue jeans and scuffed black shoes.

'Molly,' said the man in a deep voice.

'How do you know my name?' I whispered - scared. Then thoughts came rushing into my head. What should I do? Why did I go through the woods? What's going to happen to me? I tried to scream, but he covered my mouth. His hands smelt of cigarettes, I started coughing.

'Shut up and listen, if you tell anyone what I am going to tell you and make you do, then . . . I'll kill you. This is what I want you to do . . .' his voice trailing away . . .

Charlotte Wright (11)
Hardwick Middle School, Bury St Edmunds

The Hitchhiker

I was always a hard worker, looking for challenges, trying to do my best. I was calm and quiet and never got in a mood with anyone, but that was until I was mentally scarred by a terrifying event.

Late one night I had just finished work, it was dark and pouring with rain. I got in the car, turned the key and the radio came on.

'Hi, nice of you to join us at 10 o'clock.'

I turned it off and put the wipers on full blast. I was about two miles from home when I saw a man. He was wearing a green, torn coat, he had scuffed shoes, bright blue eyes and blond, spiky hair. He looked a bit scary. I felt sorry for him (I was quite a charitable person) so I pulled over and opened the window. 'Where do you want to go?'

'I'll tell you when I get in,' his voice sounded dark and it gave me the chills.

He jumped in the car and didn't put on a seat belt. His face, which was dirty and pale, looked frightened. He then put a gun to my head (I didn't feel so charitable now) and pulled his hood over his head. I was petrified, I didn't know what to do.

'I wanna go to the bank, get me to the bank now!' This time his voice sounded different, more anxious and nervous.

I slammed down the accelerator and the car pulled away. I started screaming.

'Shut it, shut it or I'll kill you, I will, I mean it!'

The gun was shaking, I didn't know what to do. I thought I was going to die . . .

Kelsey Butcher (12)
Hardwick Middle School, Bury St Edmunds

Barrage

There were flashes in the distance, red, orange, white. They were so dazzling that you were left with a glowing imprint of them on your eyelids, long after they had stopped. The incandescent bursts of light moved inexorably closer, until it seemed that they were directly above our upturned faces.

The sound was deafening, huge thunder claps of noise that rent the peaceful night sky. A young child began to whimper in fear, but was hastily hushed by her mother. The thick smell of smoke filled the air, leaving an acrid taste in my mouth. I could hear the crackling of flames.

The jostling crowd swept this way and that and I was swept along with them on a tide of human emotion. It was the best fireworks display ever!

Amber Curtis (14)
Hethersett High School, Norwich

The Dark Reckoning

The Castellan was distracted by a sudden increase in the firing at one of the doors. Howls and yells announced an Ork attack was imminent. He crossed to it in three quick strides, just in time to meet the aliens' rush. A huge Ork leader crashed through the doorway and eviscerated an Initiate with a thrust beneath his breastplate.

Sefran parried its next blow and countered with a swing perfectly timed to catch his foe off balance from his missed attack. The glittering energy field of his ancient power sword slashed through the Ork's neck with barely a hint of resistance and the great Ork fell, clutching spasmodically at the stump of its neck.

Sefran leapt forward into the lesser Ork's behind, hacking and slashing with little finesse but horrible effectiveness. Limbs and heads flew apart. In seconds the doorway was filled with twitching corpses. Brother Mikael came up with his flamer and the surviving Orks were driven back down the corridor by a wall of flames.

'The charge is prepared,' called Brother Hexil.

Sefran instantly switched comm-channels with nerve impulse. 'Castellan Sefran to Light of Purity, immediate recovery - code blue.'

The Templars moved to the centre of the chamber and were teleported to the waiting strike vessel in a blinding flash of light. Seconds later, the thermic charge blasted a new crater in the flank of the Ork space hulk.

Richard Smales (15)
Kingsbrook School, Milton Keynes

One Night In The Life Of A Fox

Dear Diary,

Tonight was a scary one. I went to Full-Of-Food Farm to find some rabbits in Grumpy-Old-Man's field. But Long-Tongue, Big-Nose, Floppy-Ears and Tail-Burned-By-Firework (his hounds) woke up Grumpy-Old-Man and he got out his instant death-stick and started firing at me! Good grief, I was only after some rabbits! Those humans are so annoying, they hunt me and my family for fun and when I try to find some little bunnies, that don't even belong to them, they try to blast my head off.

So, as you can imagine, as soon as I saw Grumpy-Old-Man coming I ran for the hills. As well as firing his instant death-stick at me he set his hounds on me. Talk about a bad night!

Luckily I managed to shake off Grumpy-Old-Man, Long-Tongue and Tail-Burned-By-Firework at Falling Water Hill but Big-Nose and Floppy-Ears were still after me. So I went into Full-Of-Trees-Place and darted in and out of the trees until Big-Nose gave up, but Floppy-Ears was still after me. So as I ran past, All-The-Way-Round-Sight flew down to distract him while I ran to my den.

Well, it's almost morning. Goodnight

From
Red-As-Cherries.

Lara Sadler (12)
Kingsbrook School, Milton Keynes

A Cat's Night Out

Dear Diary,

Last night was unfair. I was happily catnapping in my triangular bed when my owner threw me out. Suddenly the box thing went dark. There's no turning back! It was up to me to survive the night.

I thought, where do I start? Oh right I know. I will catch a mouse or maybe a rabbit. *Zoom, zoom!* A mouse! I was off! Darting in and out the fresh green grass, *snap!* Got it! Wait a minute! It wasn't a mouse I'd just bitten into? It was! *Miaow!* Oh no, the street-hard, punk cat. His name is Razor, but everyone calls him Scarface. He has been in so many fights, half of both his ears are gone.

I must have been knocked out. The last thing I remember was the revolting smell of Scarface's breath.

I woke up finally. I was safe in my owner's arms, Well that is it! I went hungry all night. I caught no mice, but at least I was safe.

Abbie Stock (11)
Kingsbrook School, Milton Keynes

A Day In The Life Of Anne Frank

(A possible missing diary entry?)

Dear Kitty

Oh how I tire of being in hiding! I can see the Dutch children playing from outside my window. They have nothing, but they are free.

I really can't stand the company. At dinner tonight we were discussing what we would do if we were let out of hiding today. I said the first thing I would do is run. Anywhere, I would just run. Mrs Vann Dann said I should have a more sensible goal with my life. That I should crave more at 14 than to run. Apparently I should have said that the first thing I would do, is try to find some suitable aim for my life. Like perfect Margot, who said she would find work in a business. But I do not care for such trivial things. For me, I crave freedom more than anything else.

I've been in hiding now for nearly a year. That's a year since I've ran, jumped or even felt the cool air on my face. Things I took for granted a year ago. Once I step out into the great outdoors I shall not go off immediately and find dull work. I shall enjoy the year I lost up here, before I try to find someone to publish this diary. I heard they're looking for war diaries. I would love to be a journalist though. To travel the world in search of the most romantic and adventurous places on Earth.

I cannot stand Margot at times. Everyone loves her. I don't. Not always.

Amy Sellman-Bartlett (13)
Kingsbrook School, Milton Keynes

Forbidden Siren

It was a dark night in the town of Bloodville, when all of a sudden there was an earthquake and then there were a load of screams coming from the village, so I (Ben Connor) went to the town square to see what had happened. 'Oh man! What is that?'

It was a dead person walking towards me. It looked like it had been shot and stabbed. 'Blood! Blood!' it said.

I found a fire poker in a pile of ashes. I stabbed it six times but it just kept coming so I ran away as fast as I could, when all of a sudden I bumped into someone.

'Hi, my name is John Betts, I am one of the survivors.'

I said, 'Let's go!'

We ran for our lives. We eventually found a little house. We went in and looked about.

'I've found a gun,' I shouted, 'come on let's go and kill some zombies!'

We left with our guns and flame throwers. We found the village.

'Look out behind you!'

Bang! Bang! Bang!

'I think it's dead, Connor.'

'Yeah, let's get out of here!'

We went into a police station and there was a zombie staring at me right in the eyes, but he didn't have any eyes. I pulled out my gun and blew his head off. We found a telephone and rang the army and managed to get out alive.

Earth had to be aborted. The army nuked it.

Tony Gallop (13)
Kingsbrook School, Milton Keynes

A Day In The Life Of The Boy Band Blue

(In the view of Antony Costa)

I was woken up this morning by our tour manager. We are playing live at Wembley and our new album is released today. 'Guilty' is our third album, along with 'All Rise' and 'One Love'. Also, Lee Ryan is going to face the press today as he is going to court after beating up two photographers. Duncan James is moving in with his new girlfriend and Simon Webbe has just found a new love. I am getting back together with my ex-wife Lucy to look after our new baby girl Emily.

We're just about to go into wardrobe, hair and make-up to shoot our latest video, 'Breathe Easy'. In this video, Lee is the main singer and it is very cold outside. There is snow lying around and we talk about not being able to live without a special girl. Duncan is talking to our choreographer.

'Breathe easy.' We have just finished singing and are making our way to the coach so we can get to Wembley. At last we arrive at Wembley and get ready for the show tonight.

'Thank you everyone, we love you!' Duncan, Lee, Simon and me shout to the crowds.

That was the end of the tour. Being in a boy band is hard work, but good fun.

That was a day in the life of 'Blue'.

Lauren Saunders (11)
Kingsbrook School, Milton Keynes

It's Not Everything You Want

Famous people always seem to have everything - money, cars, big houses, swimming pools, massive gardens - but expensive things can't make you happy forever.

In my story I'm going to be taking a look at a person who seems happy on the outside but not so much on the inside.

A day in the life of Vanessa Roberts. She's beautiful, tall, slim, with long blonde hair, bright blue eyes and excellent facial features. What more could you ask for?

(Alarm clock goes off.)

'Wake up Vanessa, it's time to go to the gym. Your new instructor Kirsten Spears is there. I've heard she's the best!' Chad excitedly told her. (Chad is her helper, he helps her with the timetable and what she does.)

'Yeah, yeah, coming,' she shouted to Chad. She started whispering to herself, '6.30 in the morning with a long day ahead, recording my new ad, wait, I can't go out looking like this . . . '

'Chad, where's my wardrobe and make-up artist!' Vanessa shouted her head off to Chad.

'Sorry we're late, it's just the traffic was heavy even though it's so early!' apologised the make-up artist. 'So what do you want?'

'My usual,' replied Vanessa.

Her make-up took 10 minutes because she didn't need lots but by then she was late for her gym class. She couldn't get everything right. Inside she felt so tired and unhappy because wherever she went, there were cameras. She couldn't even get a normal boyfriend.

The rest of the day she would just get bossed around, never allowed to do what she wanted, always what they wanted.

Natasha Toms (11)
Kingsbrook School, Milton Keynes

Dragon Queen

'She lives deep in the rainforest.'

'Who does?' said a girl.

'The Dragon Queen,' replied the chief.

We were sitting in the shade of a monkey puzzle tree talking about why we worship dragons.

'What does the queen look like?' I asked.

'She has black hair that reaches her heels.'

'And?' I asked, enjoying the legend.

'She has gold eyes and red lips and brown skin.'

'What else?' asked a boy.

'She has dragons with her all the time.'

'Wow!' My mouth fell open. 'Dragons!'

'Yes she saved Africa from a deadly animal,' said the chief.

'How?' asked my brother, dropping his orange.

'Well I was walking down by the river and . . .'

'What?' Everyone leaned closer, listening to every word.

'The dragons closed around the animal and it was never seen again.'

Everyone gaped open-mouthed. I looked up from the trees and saw a woman standing on a dragon. She waved and vanished.

Kathryn Jenkins (12)
Kingsbrook School, Milton Keynes

Untitled

I had to wake up early to go to his house. I got dressed and set off on my horse. I went through forests and along the countryside. It was a hard, long journey but I got there in the end.

I kept knocking on the door but no one answered so I made my way back. I went past the cemetery and went in to have a look. I was looking around and out of the corner of my eye I saw the name, *Douglas Morris* on a grave.

I had travelled all this way for £200 to find the person who owes me the money is dead!

Scott Winkworth (12)
Kingsbrook School, Milton Keynes

Murderer

It was a long time ago. I remember it as if it were yesterday. The blood, the tears, the screams, directed at me. 'Murderer, murderer,' they used to chant. They used to spit on me in the streets, kick me in the road and graffiti my property.

I was young and a newlywed when the attack happened. I loved my husband greatly but he didn't try. He was very popular in our village. We argued day in, day out and people used to hear. That's why they blamed me . . .

It was a cold, rainy morning, the usual weather in Lower Stockham in the Lake District. I woke with a headache and went back to bed. John was downstairs. I woke later to the sound of John crying, 'Gladys, Gladys, help!'

I ran downstairs and found John, dead, on my kitchen floor. I ran to him and tried to stop the bleeding but it was too late. He was dead. My hands were bloodstained and as I picked up the knife that had killed the man I loved most in the world, the neighbours swung the door open.

I could see the horror in their eyes. They saw a man whom they had loved very much, dead - with his wife, bloodstained and red-eyed, holding a dagger.

They rang the hospital and police. I tried to tell them, screamed at them, that I did nothing. Why would I kill my husband? But no one believed me.

I am desperate to know who killed him to clear my name. Please John, show them it wasn't me, show them the real murderer . . .

Rebecca Haigh (11)
Kingsbrook School, Milton Keynes

A Man At My Door

January 16th 1849:

I woke up in a panic this morning. I couldn't believe I had fallen asleep on the day the traveller was coming to look for me. 18 years ago this day I was murdered, shot in the back by a traveller.

I was walking home from the pub and there he sat. I said, 'Good day old chap,' as I walked by. I walked another yard or so and *bang!* I was shot dead.

Ever since that day I have haunted that man and every January 16th I scare the living daylights out of him. I move things around his caravan, let his horse off his lead and make him run away. But last year I went too far, I stole his caravan. This year he has come looking for it. I may be dead but I have my weaknesses and he knows them.

He will come on the strike of midnight and kill me once more. You may think it is impossible but he can kill my soul every night. I come alive and die when the light shines, so he can shoot me again if I do not hide.

Bang, bang! That's him, he is standing by my door. I'm too scared to answer. Maybe if I hide he will go away or maybe he will come back another day. *Bang, bang!* (again). Will he go away?

I hear a note coming through the door. I pick it up and it reads, 'Don't forget I am after you and I intend to kill you'.

Adam Lambert (13)
Kingsbrook School, Milton Keynes

The Beginning Of The Apocalypse

An everyday village event turned into a baffling disaster!

The village of Littleham, an ideal, rural area with plenty of interesting history, hasn't seen so much action since the bombing of 1944.

It holds a race every year in memory of lives lost in the Second World War, but yesterday things turned upside down and scientists are saying, 'This is not physically possible!' Contenders in the race were lost because the ground opened up and swallowed everyone running.

Eye-witness, Kate Serfield (race organiser and wife of contender) said, 'My husband has run the race for six years and never has anything so terrible occurred! I have been assured that a team of qualified diggers will dig up the exact spot where it happened! I will never help organise the race again and I doubt it will be on next year anyway!'

Eye-witnesses tell us the ground 'lifted, revealing lava underneath' and 'moved so quickly, the runners didn't have time to dodge out of its way'.

Some believe that Devil worship around the area in the middle ages has provoked the Devil to kill remaining links to used to be non-believers but spiritual and religious sceptics call this theory irrational.

Intense surveys of the area are being carried out to help scientists draw out sensible conclusions.

A skilled geographical scientist, John Cooley, believes. 'This is a similar occurrence to an earthquake where two of the Earth's plates overlap and move but with surprising results' - but how come it has never happened before?

Experts are baffled, locals scared and believers in religion are turning to their god. We aren't even sure if the people who were swallowed are still alive.

One thing is for sure, the villagers never want it to happen again.

This is *The Daily Shout Out* - we will always keep you up to date.

Emily Weissang (11)
Kingsbrook School, Milton Keynes

A Mechanical Feature

Over the seven seas and far away lived a little boy. He lived with his mother in a small farmhouse in the country. The area was quiet and all green, the only thing was the rabbit hole at the end of the garden, with the rabbit scratching now and then. His favourite thing was the tall oak tree, that caused him more trouble than he had imagined.

'Happy birthday to you, happy birthday to you, happy birthday dear Ben, happy birthday to you.'

Ben and his mum were in the kitchen it was Ben's birthday. He was 12 today but did not seem very pleased about it. There was nobody to play with, all he wanted was a friend. He went outside, feeling down, to see the old oak tree. He climbed high. As he jumped down, there was a noise, *'Achoo!'* Something was in the tree. Then it happened again. Ben looked inside the tree, but nothing. He looked round the back of the tree and saw a mechanical feature. 'Hello,' it said, 'my name's T4B4.'

Ben looked a bit surprised, he had never seen anything like it before.

Ben's mum came outside to see Ben, when she saw T4B4. 'I'll phone the police,' she whispered.

'No don't,' Ben shouted.

'Have I done something wrong?' asked T4B4.

'No, she just doesn't know you,' answered Ben.

In the next hour the police arrived and Ben's mum explained what she could. All the time T4B4 was hiding. Just then T4B4 sneezed, again. *'Achoo.'*

'T4B4?' called the officer.

'Yes?' he said. 'Oops.'

'Come out, Mr Mechnac is looking for you.'

'But.'

'No buts, let's go.'

By the next hour they were gone and there was nobody to play with Ben again.

'Oh well,' he said, 'it was fun.'

'Maybe you'll see him again.'

'Maybe.'

Then there was a sound and a little mechanical voice whispered, 'Ben . . .'

Clare Booth (11)
Kingsbrook School, Milton Keynes

Pirates Attack City

It was last night the sea was rough and the winds extremely blustery. The tide came in on the coast of Norwich. A local businessman, who lives opposite the beach, was thought to have awoken by the noise of lapping waves on the rocks.

They were carrying cutlasses, daggers and a tall, broad man with only one leg (their leader) carrying five pistols. In all there were 27 of them.

They were here for valuables and there has been no deaths. Another witness has got a photo of this so-called Jolly Roger in his shop.

This all happened at midnight last night and there has been a warning they might strike again as they have been attacking all over Europe.

Ben Keen-Toombs (11)
Kingsbrook School, Milton Keynes

The Mystery

As Bob walked through the jungle he tripped over.

Bob was on the lookout for treasure. He got up and carried on walking. Then he heard a strange noise. He started to approach the noise that was out in the bush.

As he got near he saw a body lying dead on the floor. It had a cut throat. He didn't like the look of it so he turned back and headed off into the bush. He was now scared. He'd totally forgotten about the treasure.

Then he heard another noise. He didn't bother to look this time. Ten minutes later he came to a clearing in the jungle. He was very close to the treasure. He walked to where the treasure was.

He found the exact spot, and had a drink. Then he started to dig.

He dug down a foot deep and then, as he looked up, he had a knife through his throat. All he saw was blood. The killer had gone. He didn't see anybody, just blood.

By this time he was half-dead. He crawled over to a tree to try and pull himself up, but he couldn't. Later he was dead. He had died of blood loss. The killer will remain a mystery.

Daniel Welch (12)
Kingsbrook School, Milton Keynes

The Orphan Girl

There once was a girl called Jenni that lived in an orphanage. She used to get really badly bullied by the other children because she had three eyes. All the children laughed in her face and wouldn't go near her. Some of them just completely ignored her and acted like she wasn't even there at all. Lots of people looked around the orphanage looking to adopt or foster. But when they saw Jenni they just turned up their noses and carried on walking.

One day another person came into the orphanage. His name was John. This boy was the same age as Jenni. When he walked in the children all burst out laughing because he was a bit plump and had big metal braces that came up over his head. He also wore glasses. But Jenni didn't find it funny. She went over to the boy and introduced herself. 'Hello I'm Jenni. Don't take any notice of them they're just mean; they do that to me too,' she told him.

A couple of days later when they got to know each other really well somebody came in to adopt two children. Neither of them thought they would get picked so they just sat down in silence. The two people got to them and looked at each other and said, 'Ahh look at them they are so sweet.' The pair walked off down to the office. When they came back they picked up the children, Jenni and John, and took them home with them.

Kayleigh Whitlock (12)
Kingsbrook School, Milton Keynes

A Night In The Life Of A Panda

Hello my name is Mia Chi I'm a giant panda which means black and white foot cat and I'm going to tell you about my night (I sleep in the day. I am nocturnal.)

6pm - getting dark perfect for going out for a meal, or thirty.

7pm - I've found a lovely garden of bamboo. This keeps the old choppers busy, ooh that rat looks tasty. I do like a bit of meat now and again.

8pm - Damn that vermin, it got away, oh and here comes that Diao Ji. She thinks she owns these forests and I ain't in the mood to talk to her. Whenever I see her it's always the third degree. How's that bamboo taste? Can I have some fruit? Why? Where'd you get it? Seen any tasty rats lately?

12pm - Thank God she's gone. I thought she'd never go. Now I can carry on eating. I have to eat 300lbs of food each day and 99% of that is bamboo.

5am - Oh no dawn is coming, the light hurts my eyes. I better go and rest. Thanks for listening to my day. I'd ask you to come back but I wouldn't really want to tell you my day again, now would I?

Thomas Basketfield (12)
Kingsbrook School, Milton Keynes

Pandora's Box

There is no real version of Pandora's box. Not really. But here I sit and write the tragic tale of the dangers of the world.

Take yourself back, to the start of everything. Go up to the sky and see. There stood every god in the universe, and goddesses of course.

Penelope (a not very famous goddess) started to think, *let's make life, there's some up here but not down there.* Within minutes they had created a 'human' which they named Pandora, they used all their powers and some of themselves.

Pandora was put on Earth with a present. She was never to open the box. Pandora went for days in temptation, until one day she was so tempted she did it . . . she opened the box.

Before she knew it horrible little grey, black and green dragonflies burst out everywhere. Pandora closed the box as soon as she could. Just then she heard a teeny tiny voice. It said its name was Hope. Pandora wasn't too sure this time, but she did, she opened, once again Pandora's box.

So there you go, the untrue tale of Pandora's box. Remember don't open the box.

Sarika Patel (12)
Kingsbrook School, Milton Keynes

On Death's Doorstep

(A chapter of a story in the style of Anthony Horowitz)

He didn't see the car that hit him nor did he hear the screech of the brakes. He didn't even feel the paramedics lift him into the ambulance. But as he lay there, he opened his eyes.

'Roger,' said someone, 'it's me.'

He tried to turn over to see who had called him, but he didn't have the energy, so he just let his head fall into the pillow. Everywhere was silent, then suddenly he sat bolt upright and with a pounding heart, he gasped for air. Then he collapsed into a lifeless heap on the floor.

'Roger, are you alright?'

Then the moment his parents had been dreading. The doctor came out of the surgery and walked over to them. 'We tried everything,' the doctor spoke in a scared voice. 'All we can do now is hope and pray, and see what time will bring.'

Meanwhile in the surgery Roger had come round fully. But to Roger everything seemed like a great blur, seeing as though his glasses had been broken in the accident. 'Where am I?' he just managed to murmur.

Felicia Gatenby (12)
Kingsbrook School, Milton Keynes

American Express - Street Fire In Orlando

There was a terrible incident involving fire in Orlando, yesterday morning. An Al Quaedal petrol bomber was lurking in the back streets of Orlando, USA, in the early hours of yesterday morning. The fire occurred when a now - imprisoned terrorist blew up a house next to a gas station. He killed a family of nine in the house and 16 people at the gas station.

The gas station imploded and caused a massive chain fire. A huge amount of people died, (about 40,000) according to investigators.

Families in other countries are just finding out. This is a quote from one of the families: 'I can't believe this has happened. She'd only just come to visit me and when she went back this happened. I just hope justice is brought in court, and filthy men like that aren't allowed to roam the streets'.

Investigators are still looking for the bodies of 2,000 people who are thought to have been there at that time. Scientists aren't just worried about people, they estimate that 30,000 dogs died in the blaze. One scientist claimed: 'This event could dangerously decrease the population of pets in America'. Orlando is the main breeding ground and home for most common pets.

Kieran Price (11)
Kingsbrook School, Milton Keynes

Mum?

(A chapter in the style of Jacqueline Wilson)

I've always known my mum was out there somewhere, but any notions of finding her were stomped out by Karen (my dad's obnoxious girlfriend). She relished in telling me how my mum died when I was young. She would spit, rolling her tongue around every word. When I was little I used to flinch in the corner, but by the time I was 12 I learned to stand up for myself, which made her slap me even more. Dad doesn't dare to stand up to her. He just busies himself in the kitchen or something. Anyway, back to the story.

It was my 13th birthday and, as usual, nobody acknowledged my presence. So I went up in the attic to sulk (as I do). I decided to keep busy, so I started to sort through some old boxes of junk. I was through about the sixth box when a bundle of letters caught my eye. They were for me! One for every birthday. I sifted through the pile until I found the thirteenth one. I ripped it open and read anxiously.

'Dear Ruby,

Sorry I can't be with you. You see, I have cancer and don't have long to live. But just at my darkest days, your smile would always cheer me up. You're a teenager now! I thought I'd write a letter for each birthday for you to remember me by. Don't give your dad too much trouble! I love you always, Mum xxx'

I just sat there as the tears welled up and spilled over.

Rebecca Houseago (11)
Kingsbrook School, Milton Keynes

Harry Potter

Harry was just about to walk to his car when Tonks said, 'Harry watch yourself.' Harry just ignored her and kept on walking. Harry looked round to wave at them but found them all looking just above his head, their mouths open. He turned around slowly and could not believe his eyes. Right in front of him was Malfoy riding a dragon. Harry pulled out his wand but Malfoy had already got his out and was shooting red and white pieces of light at Harry. He moved out of the way and quickly shot some curses back at him, but the dragon blocked Malfoy from getting hurt.

Harry was now in panic, there was no one to help him. Harry wished someone would come. Then, without realising, Harry muttered something under his breath and all he saw was the dragon blow up, there was no sign of Malfoy anywhere. Harry thought he had killed Malfoy.

Matthew Leach (11)
Kingsbrook School, Milton Keynes

Good And Evil

There was a boy called Jim. He lived on his own because his mum and dad got killed in a car crash. He was happy living on his own. He often paid visits down the churchyard. He didn't want to live with his nan and grandad or any other relations because he wanted to live in the house his mum and dad used to live in. He always cried when he got home from school.

One evening Jim was on his way home from school. He called in the churchyard and he saw that all of the gravestones were knocked over apart from his mum and dad's ones. Jim just thought the wind had done it. Jim went home.

The next evening Jim was late going down to the churchyard (very late). He heard the clock strike twelve. It was frosty and the moon was shining brightly, the grass had a silver shine on it, the gravestone was shining brightly too. Jim heard a noise then he looked up. He saw six ghosts. These ghosts were nice, kind and caring. They told him that when he died he would be up there with them. Jim was gobsmacked.

There was a loud noise then there were these ugly ghosts. The kind ghosts hid behind a tree. The ugly, evil and uncaring ghosts killed Jim with one blow. Jim turned into a ghost but he belonged to the evil group. Jim decided to go and join the nice group. Then everyone became friends - the evil ghosts, who now were good ghosts, told him that when they got angry they knocked the gravestones over but left his mum and dad's so it didn't upset him.

The next night they put the gravestones back up.

Nicola Welch (12)
Kingsbrook School, Milton Keynes

Underwater Adventure

One day when I was walking home from school I started to feel very hot and dizzy. I could feel a pain in my leg so I looked to see what it was. It was a tooth in my leg. The tooth caused me to fall to the ground.

The next thing I knew was that I was underwater swimming. It was amazing because I could breathe underwater. It was very weird. I started to get scared though because I didn't know where I was or how I got there. So I asked a fish where I was. The fish was very mean and he called his friends over and they were gong to eat me, I was terrified.

The only option I had was to try and fight them. All of a sudden I was given a boost of strength. Then I shot laser beams from my eyes and killed every single fish and there was about seven of them.

Three days later I was still underwater. The only food I had was some seaweed. Then I met a fish called Bryan. He told me there was no way out and I would have to live the rest of my life underwater. But as I was swimming I bumped my head on a big, sharp rock. Then I found myself lying in an alley. I thought it must have all been a dream but I found a cut in my leg which looked like a tooth mark.

Sam White (12)
Kingsbrook School, Milton Keynes

Code Voronica: X

Bang! Bang! went the door opposite Claire Redfield. Claire was from Racconn City, just before it was destroyed by the T-virus. The T-virus was a bio-weapon created by Unbrealer to kill people and turn them into zombies. Claire left Racconn City to look for her brother, Chris. He was stolen by Unbrealer and taken to a prison island also wrecked by the T-virus.

Bang! Bang! the door was still being smashed. It was a group of zombies that were smashing the door down. Claire, at the moment, was on the prison island. *Swoosh!* The door went flying off. Claire pulled out a handgun and jumped in the air backwards and pulled the trigger. Everything went in slow-motion as she pulled the trigger again and again. You could hear the shells tapping the floor. The zombies kept coming, she was outnumbered, she ran into the next room, she re-loaded her gun and she turned around. *Drip, dri,p, drip* was all she heard at that moment. She turned around to find a puddle of blood on the floor. Claire looked up! It was a licker! A licker was a zombie but a different breed. A licker was a person who had the T-virus injected straight into their bloodstream. A licker could crawl up walls and had a long, razor blade tongue with sharp teeth and claws. Then Claire remembered that lickers were blind. So she took little footsteps to the next room.

In the next room Chris Redfield was being watched by zombie dogs, Claire pulled out a gun and shot them all. Chris planted a bomb. They ran out, jumped into a helicopter and got away in time . . .

Zac White
Kingsbrook School, Milton Keynes

Alex Rider

(In the style of Anthony Horowitz)

Alex stared at the cell door that had just shut in his face. He pressed the alarm on his watch three times and out came a thin piece of metal about 10cm long. Although the door was six inches of thick steel he identified the lock as a weakness. Alex poked the piece of metal down the keyhole and felt for a little catch. The door swung open.

A guard was standing at the end of the hall. Alex knew he would have to move quickly if he was going to be able to disarm the bomb. He ran speedily but silently, on his toes at all times, towards the guard. Alex lashed out with a strong blow to the ribs and followed up with an elbow to the head. This left the man unconscious. Alex sprang up taking the steps three at a time. He glanced at his watch. He only had five minutes before the bomb was due to go off. If he didn't get there in time the whole of London would be ash. Alex knew the bomb was strapped to the table in the dining room. He was getting nearer. Just one corner to go.

'What are you doing?' Dr Grief snarled whilst standing in front of five guards.

'I'm doing my job!'

Alex ran as fast as he could to Dr Grief. Grief fired three bullets. One skimmed Alex's shoulder. He didn't care. He ran, jumped. *Smack!* Alex hit Dr Grief full throttle in the face. Grief didn't even flinch. A bit of blood trickled down his nose.

'Get him!'

One of the men swung a foot towards him. Alex blocked and then struck back with a counter. This knocked the man back into another. The largest of the guards flung a right hook at Alex. Alex ducked and swept his foot across the floor. The guard fell to the ground. Alex rolled past one guard and drove his hand into the man's back. Alex fell to the floor to dodge a dangerous punch and raised his elbow into the puncher's knee. He fell. Alex stood up to see Dr Grief pointing a gun at his chest. He looked at a gadget on his arm.

'You have one minute left Alex Rider. You have annoyed me too long so I have come to the conclusion of killing you.'

Max Ikin (12)
Kingsbrook School, Milton Keynes

A Day In The Life Of Alan Shearer

Being a famous footballer is every child's dream, it was my dream too, when I was a child and my dream came true, I, Alan Shearer, became Newcastle's captain.

Beep, beep, beep, beep, beep, beep. See our lives aren't full of glitz and glamour, even famous people need alarm clocks. How else would we wake up? Every day around half seven my alarm clock wakes me up and I struggle getting out of bed. I get in the shower, wash my hair and get dressed. I go downstairs and have breakfast, normally pancakes, then I go upstairs and clean my teeth. I leave the house and head to St James' Park. I train on Mondays, Tuesdays, Thursdays, Fridays and sometimes Sundays. I park my silver Bentley in my parking spot and head to the changing rooms.

Only me and Bramble get changed there, everyone else got ready at home. Today's match day. We're playing Ipswich. Bramble, Bellamy and Roberts are on the bench for the first half and the rest of us are playing.

We head towards the pitch through the tunnel, Ipswich are already out there. We start with the ball, Bramble takes it down the pitch and passes it to Roberts, Roberts shoots and hits the crossbar, goal kick, the ball lands right at my feet. I take it down the pitch and I get ready to shoot but I get tackled, staggering pain spreads in my leg, the paramedics carry me off the pitch. Will I ever play again?

Ashleigh Hall (12)
Kingsbrook School, Milton Keynes

A Day In The Life Of A Pirate

As I woke up in my attic room on my birthday, 8th of June, I had a strange feeling in my mind. I ran downstairs and met my mum and sister in the kitchen, where I excitedly blew out my birthday cake candles and made a wish.

Shortly after I made my wish a message appeared on top of my cake, it read:

'A pirate's life is a life for me,
Yo, ho, ho and a bottle of rum,
Travelling on the big wide sea,
Yo, ho, ho and a bottle of rum'.

After I had read the message a green whirlwind formed around me, and dropped me on a pirate ship. I spent the afternoon making friends with the pirates, and that evening the ship was attacked.

I feared for my life and hid in the nearest thing that I could see, an empty barrel. I swivelled and turned to stop myself from getting hit by the swords that consistently were stabbed into the barrel. Soon all became quiet so I peeked out of the top of the barrel and . . . the message appeared on the floor just like on the cake and a green whirlwind formed around me again and took me back home.

When I got home no time had passed, I told my mum and sister my story, then we ate the cake!

Emma Cumberlidge (11)
Kingsbrook School, Milton Keynes

Pirates' Pleasure

Pirates destroy all of the town's properties.

Today was a terrible tragedy. The treacherous pirates have killed, tortured and destroyed most of Milton Keynes! This terrible crime first started at 10 o'clock last night and carried on through the night. It was a cold and shivering day and for this attack to occur has made the day a whole lot worse. If you walk through the ancient town of Milton Keynes you would not recognise it at all, burning houses, over 200 police and civilians helping to uncover dead bodies and some that are still alive.

We are standing here in Milton Keynes and I am just about to speak to Ben Dover who has lost a family in this terrible tragedy. 'So Ben how do you feel? Do you feel frightened about this?'

'Well of course I have just lost my mum. They tore her legs off and then . . . then ate her!'

'Ohh.'

'I know I feel like I want to kill myself. Well I don't want this tragedy to ever happen again but I don't know how the pirates even came over here.'

Matthew Krzywon (12)
Kingsbrook School, Milton Keynes

Untitled

When Liz woke she found herself in a hammock covered by a sheepskin blanket. She sat up and she sat on something sharp, it was a spoon. *Why would a spoon be in my hammock?* thought Liz.

Liz was 10 years old but acted like an 8-year-old. She got up and put the spoon into an empty bowl lying on the floor near the floorboard that was abandoned on the grassy land. She sat down on the damp grass she sat pretending to be eating breakfast. She sat there then suddenly a pink mouse, (her favourite) appeared in the bowl - she eagerly ate it and pretended more and more appeared in the bowl but this time it was melted chocolate. She ate it slowly this time and it trickled down her face. She then went exploring.

She bent down looking at a pixie, it was wearing a blue skirt, a yellow top and little brown clogs. It also had wings. It flew onto Lizzy's hand and sat there staring into her eyes. It got up and flew away.

She reached a tree and it had a door in it. There was a *Break Time* sign on the door. She could hear screaming music from inside it. She knocked on the door. A fat boy opened the door. He looked at her then said, 'Who are you?'

Then Liz said, 'More to the point who are you and where am I? Is this some kind of a joke?'

Food appeared in bowls and pixies sat on Lizzy's hand. 'Surely this is a joke?'

'I'm Bruce and this is Whateverland, no it's not a joke, so stop asking questions and enjoy yourself!'

Amiee Read (12)
Kingsbrook School, Milton Keynes

Treasure Island: The Capture Of The Pirate And Treasure

Smollet: Don't just let him get away with it. Get the boat upright again and let's chase him.

Trelawny: Jim stay here and help these men push the boat while me and Dr Livesy get into the little boat and we'll pull once we've tied this rope here to the cannon up there.

Dr Livesy: Ready. Heave!

Jim: Yes, straight in one.

Smollet: Everyone on board. Put up the sails. We must chase him down quickly.

Trelawny: Good work, let's get going.

Adult Jim: So there I was on the Hispaniola searching for Silver.

(Now we join Silver on his boat.)

Silver: Seems to have got bouncy over the last few minutes but don't worry treasure I won't let you go. What was that . . . ?

Parrot: Cannonball! Cannonball!

Silver: Cannonball! How did that get here? Damn blast them to come look for my treasure.

Smollet: Move up beside him. I need to talk to him.

First sailor: Yes Captain.

Smollet: Get a move on with it then. Good day Silver, we've come for . . .

Silver: The gold. Well you can't have it. It's mine and Parrot's here.

Parrot: Pieces of eight, pieces of eight.

Smollet: Get him!

All sailors: Yes Captain!

Trelawny: Fire!

Silver: Don't shoot!

Trelawny: Deal with it.

(Silver jumps into the water.)

Smollet: You get that treasure, and you.

All: Yes we've done it, we've got the treasure.

Elliott Nichols (12)
Kingsbrook School, Milton Keynes

Spheres

What do you think would happen if the whole world went completely out of balance? Well this is what happens to Lisa Sanders on a trip to save the world.

On her way to the Orange Islands, Lisa noticed a sudden change in the weather as she crossed the border to the Orange Islands. The waves crashed against the rocks of the islands, she was carried by the waves to one of the four balanced islands. People in strange costumes said that they needed her help in collecting three spheres from the other three balanced islands, but what Lisa didn't know was, guarding the spheres were three creatures of great power.

On her journey to the islands, she met the creatures. The creatures were distracted by something in the air that captured one of the creatures. Lisa sneaked past and onto one of the islands and found the first sphere. She crept to the second island and found the second sphere but was forced to go back to the island he landed on, by the creatures.

She placed the two spheres in place and went to the final island and found the final sphere and was about to go back to the main island when the legendary creature, the beast of the sea, was forced to the surface. It grabbed Lisa and carried her to the main island to place the sphere and balance everything out once again. The captured creature was released, became legendary again and Lisa returned home.

Lilly Mercer (11)
Kingsbrook School, Milton Keynes

Bullied To Death

(By Emily Corso's Mum)

When Emily was alive, she was a great kid, loving, kind and caring. Also Emily was very clever. She used to be bullied at school and I tried everything but it would not stop. While Emily was being bullied she was beaten up too, which scared me, I tried to sort that out as well.

One day (11th January 2003) Emily went back to school from half term. While she was at school in the morning she was beaten up near the school gates. Then at lunchtime Emily was punched and kicked on her body, but worst of all was after school when the bullies beat Emily to her death. I found her there 1-2 hours later, she was stone cold.

The bullies will live to regret it. I really miss my darling Emily. Remember never be a bully and destroy lives.

Advice About Bullying

If you are being bullied don't worry we'll help you.

Tell them you don't care and ignore them, they'll soon get bored.

Tell a teacher.

Ring Childline for more advice.

Sophie Pettifer (11)
Kingsbrook School, Milton Keynes

The Mystery Lane

'At last we're here, hopefully this will be a peaceful holiday break.'

'Yeah. We could go sightseeing later and maybe visit the beach.'

'Cool, I'm so excited.'

'First we need to get checked in at the little hotel.'

Sharah and Clark, two college students, drove up to the little hotel.

'Sharah, help me carry the suitcases up to the hotel please.'

Sharah and Clark stumbled up the steps into the hotel.

'Hi, Clark and Sharah Brise, we have come to check in,' said Clark breathlessly.

'Ah yes, room 105, thank you, have a great holiday,' the hotel receptionist said to Clark.

The receptionist handed over the key whilst Sharah grabbed a suitcase. Clark took the key and clutched a suitcase. They walked up to their room with excitement.

'Right, what shall we do first?' questioned Clark.

'Erm, well I thought we could go sightseeing, get to know the place, we are stopping here in Texas for five weeks,' Sharah added.

They set out on a road.

'Hey wander down that lane there, I can see a bright light coming from it,' Sharah said with curiosity.

'Erm, I don't know, it looks dangerous.'

'Don't be such a chicken. Come on.'

'He is right you know, don't go down there or you will never come back!' said a faint woman walking by.

'Huh? Oh just ignore her, come on.'

'Er, OK alright.' Clark drove on down the road. The lane got darker and darker as they went on. 'I can't see the road.' Clark stopped the car and turned on the fog lights . . .

'Huuhh!' they both gasped.

The two college students were never seen again.

Stacy Pearson (12)
Kingsbrook School, Milton Keynes

Army Of The Dead

Today a stunning mass skeleton grave was revealed. It is thought to be the world's biggest and most expensive find in history.

There were two million bodies found in an underground cave and strangely had a huge number of solid gold items, estimated at £7 million worth.

After further examination they found that the bodies were once all stitched together, but most of the rope had decayed away.

All 2 million bodies were facing north with spears gripped in their hands and had been coated in some strange material making them sadly impossible to find out what era they were from.

The gold items were traced from all over the world with most of them with carvings of wars and skeletons projecting a figure with wings and a halo.

When the archaeologists dug further into the cave they found an unharmed skeleton sitting in a jewel encased chair holding a sword . . .

Jordan Eborall (11)
Kingsbrook School, Milton Keynes

Going Over

Water, dripping through the roof.
Wind, whistling through the thin walls.
Gunshots, blaring overhead.
And all the time, just sitting here.
Shells, exploding over sparse land.
Needle, poking in, out, in, out . . .
Cries heard, shots fired, a living, breathing Hell above us.
And here I am.
Just . . . sitting here.
But that's what it's like, isn't it? It's in the job description: extreme
boredom followed by violent death. Not that there was a job
description, of course. It's just what we have to do . . . leave them all.
I've got a wife back home, and two boys.
Serving king and country, they said.
It'll be over soon, they told us. Yeah right!
I've been sewing. It's a poor excuse for something to occupy our time.
It's 'The Great War'.
Don't know what's so great about it, mind you . . . all this time we've
been here and got barely any further . . .
Oh God.
I hear them calling us now. I knew it was coming; sooner or later it
does.
They tell us it's our duty. They say we owe it to the country that's fed us
and grown us up but most of my living's been done in this trench
anyway, so . . .
They tell us it's time and wish us good luck but we know we're all
dead.
And we're lined up and ready and the whistle's blown and . . .
I can barely believe I'm going to die, right here and now.
It's 10.59, 11th November 1918 . . . we go over the top.

Lauren Mooney (13)
Kingsley Park Middle School, Northampton

The Thing

Boom! Boom! Thunder plays its drums, lightning pokes its ground, the moon howls. Images run from eye to eye. My heart . . . gone! Rain crying, street lamps flickering. Help! I'm gone! I look into a puddle but is that me? Its purple eyes, its yellow, spotty face, its green hair, its . . . its . . . its . . . drop! I drop to the floor in seconds, pounding in my head and beating in my chest. I didn't know what was happening for at least half an hour.

I woke . . . in bed? Mum had brought me cornflakes and let me have hot chocolate. I didn't know what had happened when I walked to the shops last night but there is only one way to find out. I'm going . . . tonight.

I tried to sit up but, *ow!* My back! I must have done something to my back last night. My bedclothes laid over me like open arms, enclosed around me, cuddling me for protection. My pillow clamped to my head, as if it would fall off any moment now. My clothes were on me. They were cold, wet, holes were all over. It wasn't me lying in bed was it?

Everything running through my head. Should I tell Mum? Should I tell Amy? Is this thing trying to haunt me? I didn't know what to do apart from be ready tonight!

Ellis Keirle (11)
Latimer Community Arts College, Barton Seagrave

The Yeti - Myths And Legends

Heard the one about the yeti killing the prime minister? I haven't either. But I have heard of the yeti capturing three explorers and then eating them up in its cave.

It happened on the 25th January 1776. The explorers were in the Himalayas trying to get to the top of all of the mountains in a month. They had reached the halfway point of Mount Everest when they got caught in a big blizzard. While they were stumbling along, the yeti had come up behind them and grabbed them all around their waists and put them under his shoulder and walked off to his cave. You would be wondering why they hadn't seen the yeti wouldn't you? Well the yeti had come up from behind them so they wouldn't have seen it and the yeti is white and in the white snow it would have been impossible to have seen it.

The yeti took all of the explorers off to its caves and rolled a giant boulder across the cave entrance. This was when the explorers saw the yeti for the first time. It had white fluffy fur all over its body and a grey muzzle, hands and feet. It had three eyes - two at the front and one at the back of its head. You would have thought that the yeti would have eaten the explorers straight away, but he didn't, he heated up the fire and then put the explorers in a cage making them all sweat all night and most of the morning before taking them out of the cage. They were all gone in thirty seconds flat. All that was left was the bones. Rescue teams were sent out but nothing was found.

Elliott Butlin (12)
Latimer Community Arts College, Barton Seagrave

A Day In The Life Of A Soldier

March 15th 1943, time 0700 hours. The wind was in my face, I was scared, and suddenly I heard a massive whistle and bang. Quickly I unharnessed my parachute and legged it.

My first bullet went straight through a German's head. We moved forward constantly, we couldn't stay still, then the General signed, 'Make camp. Bob, church tower. volunteers for night duty? No one? OK, you do it.'

The next morning we got up before dawn. The conditions were harsh. We lived on water, beans and rice.

Suddenly we fired our Mp60s. A splash of red-hot shells fell down - *ssh.* I noticed a burning smell. A shell had fallen down my top! I quickly undid it, argh, there, it's out. *Boom!* My God the house fell down only three metres away, then rubble all over me.

Thirty-five minutes after I dug myself out, the Germans came looking. I had to do something, so quickly sharpened my comb and jumped, stabbing the first in the eyes. A German bullet shot past me. I rolled, picked up the Uzi and fired. I had to get out. On the road for ten minutes and I was already in trouble. Germans everywhere, firing.

A man stumbled past in American fatigues. 'I've crashed near the Eastern seaboard, I might be able to take off again, but my landing gear has had it.'

We ran, bullets screamed past our heads. I looked back and thought, *thank God I'm off!*

Luke Howard (12)
Latimer Community Arts College, Barton Seagrave

A Day In The Life Of My Hero!

'Goodnight Mum,' I shouted. She didn't hear, so I shouted louder, 'Goodnight!'

She finally replied, 'Goodnight.'

I looked out of the window and wished I could be my hero, (Pierce Brosnan), all because everything had gone wrong today; in dance I tripped up and smashed my knee, which throbs like mad, and . . . I got an after-school for it! I was *sooo* humiliated. I went to sleep (eventually!)

Next morning I woke up; my alarm was different! I opened my eyes with difficulty, and, to my surprise my room had altered . . . I had a different body, a different face! I had become the famous James Bond actor Pierce Brosnan! I thought it was a dream, until a beautiful young girl came in.

'Hurry up Pierce, you're going to be late for filming! Be bad if you're late!'

Somehow I thought someone was controlling me, but that couldn't be true, could it? Well I hoped not because I didn't like the sound of it! Being considered strange and all!

Once I got to the film site, I eventually realised what I was doing, I was being filmed, no scripts or anything! Argh! I was dead meat . . . until I felt like I was a puppet again. I thought it was bad, but as soon as I started talking I went blind and went back home to my own body. Phew!

Connor Hill (11)
Latimer Community Arts College, Barton Seagrave

A Day In The Life Of A Diver

If I wanted to be something I would be a deep sea diver. It would be great fun due to the adventure involved.

Up early to get down to the sea. We fly to the site and we stay on a platform which provides accommodations and a station. And we work as a team.

When we are inside the station, we discuss our strategy and where to go and if we find something we bring it back to be checked out, if it is treasure. My tasks would be to look for treasure, and bring it back.

When I dive down to the deep sea I will go down to the bottom. It is great seeing all the fish. It is fascinating, exciting but dangerous because sometimes we are away for long periods of time from home. The bad thing about it is we have to wear special suits made out of waterproof material, which also insulates the body too, so that we get the temperature. The oxygen tanks and masks are attached to our faces to make sure that we can get a good supply of oxygen when we are underwater.

We do not see anybody for weeks on end but it is better now because we can use the computer and communicate by e-mail or watch DVDs. Most times we get back we are exhausted. I enjoy this job very much because I do not know what each day will bring.

Justin Wan (12)
Latimer Community Arts College, Barton Seagrave

XIII

Jason Fly (XIII) was washed up on a beach where the lifeguard found him and took him in. She was shot down earlier, he took her knives and keys, killed some men and drove off in the jeep to Winslow Bank because he found a safe key in his pocket.

He accessed his safe and took his documents out and hit a timer. He ran away and it blew up.

Jason crawled through the hole and remembered this was his trap that he'd set to catch number 1. He killed Mr Winslow and found a tattoo on his neck with the number VIII on his neck. The FBI and the CIA had heard about this and wanted to help Jason. So they killed Colonel Mcall, number VII. Then they heard about 10 rockets about to blow with the president strapped onto one.

Jason found a doctor who was trying to kill him but Jason strangled him, he was number IIII. Afterwards he saw a man in the control room, he shot himself in the head and it opened the door and started the rockets with 10 seconds to go.

Jason ran in as fast as he could and shot all the equipment, but he heard, '4 . . . 3 . . . 2' he saw a single button he shot it, ' . . . 1 . . . sequence terminated.'

The man who'd shot himself was number II. Jason was relieved, he heard a shotgun load.

'It's time to die now Mr Fly.' The president, number 1.

Rory Tymon (11)
Latimer Community Arts College, Barton Seagrave

Mum's Advice

Sally couldn't believe it! Her, the Queen's special guest at the ball! She needed a new dress, new shoes and new haircut. 'How lucky am I?' she wondered aloud.

'Very lucky,' her mum said, 'think about it, she chose Northamptonshire, then Kettering, then Latimer, then Year 7, then your form and then you. You're very privileged.'

'I know, I wonder if she'll be really posh so I have to sit up straight, cross my legs and turn my nose to everyone?'

'No, you know what I reckon,' her mum said quietly, 'she wouldn't have picked you if she didn't like your personality and your style. I reckon she wants someone to bring her down to Earth, become a real person. Not just sitting on a throne making decisions, but going to the park to play frisbee with her corgis without being asked for an autograph. She wants to be just like you and me. So go in your trainers, jeans and a smart top and talk to her like you talk to me, that's what she wants.'

Sally looked at her mum and hugged her tight, 'OK, I'll teach her how to be normal.'

'Oh you will, I'm sure you will.'

'Mum, do you think she'll like me?'

'Did you not hear what I just said?' she said with a smile on her face.

'So, let me recap, you want me to talk slang, eat with my mouth open, and chew loudly?'

'No, just be yourself, that's all anyone can ask for.'

Christopher Marshall (12)
Latimer Community Arts College, Barton Seagrave

My Unordinary Day

I woke. Well my alarm woke me up. I got out of bed and said to my mum, who was feeding my baby brother, 'I don't feel very well.' I always try this trick with her. She just ignores me. I had tried this trick with her every day. So when I was really ill I still had to go to school.

I was walking along the road and had missed the bus to school. Not again I wish a bus would just come round that corner. Just when I reach the bus stop a bus came round the corner. This looked like a lucky day.

This was more than a lucky day. People shouted at me called me fat. I was used to this. I wish people would stop calling me fat. When I came out of my form room no one was shouting 'fat' at me. Something strange was happening. First lesson was maths. Oh no I hated maths, the teacher always picked on me because I wasn't good at maths but today he wasn't nice but did help me.

This school was a horrible school. I've told my mum but she says I'll make friends soon.

At lunch I went to the dinner hall to get lunch. I stood in the line. I would usually get pushed but I didn't. People just stood there I hadn't been recognised today. But then I think, *no, I am just dreaming it, no, it can't be.* All my dreams were coming true.

Jodie Lane (11)
Latimer Community Arts College, Barton Seagrave

A Day In The Life Of . . . Me!

In a day in the life of me I . . .

I get up in the morning at 6.50, get washed and get dressed. Then I go downstairs and get breakfast. For breakfast I have Frosties that have been in the microwave. I clean my teeth then make my bed. I spend about 15 minutes on my hair and then do my make-up. At this time it is about 7.45. I go downstairs and go on the Internet for 10 minutes, checking how many people have been on my website. At 7.55 I get ready for school. At 8.00 I leave with my friend, (Shawney). I walk to a bus stop with her and wait for my best friend Kloi. At 8.10 she comes and I walk across the cow field with her and Shawney. At 8.20 we get to school. Then at school we have two lessons then break. At break I get my lunch. Then after break I have another lesson, then lunch, then two more lessons. At 3.15 I get let out and walk to the bus stop with Kloi and Shawney. Then, with Shawney I walk down the lane and back to my house. When I get in I say hi to my mum and my dad, if he is there. I go upstairs and get changed and do my hair. When I go downstairs I talk to my mum for five minutes then go and watch TV or go out into town. If I watch TV then I watch 'Lizzie McGuire' or 'That's So Raven' on the Disney Channel.

When my mum calls me for tea I go into the kitchen and sit down, have tea and then maybe go on the Internet for an hour and speak to my friends on MSN Messenger.

At about 7.00 I go and have a bath and maybe wash my hair. After I have done that it is usually 7.30 and I go down and watch EastEnders and on Wednesday or Thursday I watch The Bill.

Usually at 9.00 I go and clean my teeth and go to bed.

That's my day!

Hannah Rush (11)
Latimer Community Arts College, Barton Seagrave

The Life Of A Victorian Girl!

Dear Cousin,

My mum and dad died when I was seven years old. From then on I have been working at a cotton wool factory. My job is to collect all the wool from where they fall on the floor. So far I've been in trouble with the master of the factory at least once every week. Usually I get half my pay if I don't work harder, but that would be painful.

All day I am on my hands and knees just waiting for my knees to start bleeding and bruising into yellow and purple patches. At night I am usually ready to sink into my bed, seeing that I have to wake at 5.30 in the morning, and at night I leave the factory at 10.00. But today has been the worst day of my life. The blisters on my hands have burst and my knees are were-flowing blood. The master of the factory smacked me with the cane because I hadn't collected all the wool that I would have done normally, but couldn't. I felt tears pricking at the back of my eyes. I lost my job straight away; he didn't even give me a chance to explain why. The reason why I am writing to you is because I have no money. So that I can do nothing at all except beg like beggars.

Your cousin, Anna.

Annika Gfrärer (12)
Linslade Middle School, Leighton Buzzard

Claudia And The Clouds

It was always sunny in Rome, the flowers were always in bloom, everyone was always happy, all apart from one goddess, Claudia.

'Get me more grapes,' Claudia shouted at her only friend. 'I am a goddess, don't disobey me, hurry up!'

Claudia wasn't a good friend, all her other friends had fallen out with her, except Ishmail. Ishmail had tried many times to get Claudia to turn into a better person, but none of her plans had worked. Ishmail was a loyal friend and felt too guilty to leave Claudia with nobody, so she stayed with her.

Ishmail fed Claudia some grapes.

'Yuck, these grapes are disgusting, do you think you have the right to feed a goddess mouldy grapes?'

'No Claudia, I'm sorry, I'll get you some fresh ones.'

So Ishmail walked to the market, many miles away, to get Claudia some fresh grapes.

Whilst Ishmail was at the market, Zeus paid a visit to Claudia. 'If you don't start to be more grateful to your only friend that hasn't left you, I will banish you far away, to where you will be alone. You will have no slave there,' Zeus said, then he vanished.

Claudia laughed, she didn't think Zeus would banish her, so she carried on treating Ishmail as if she were her slave.

Later on that night, Zeus came back. 'I warned you Claudia.' Zeus put his hand out to Claudia and shouted, 'Banish!'

Claudia whirled round and round, and then she finally fell on her feet. She had no idea where she was. It was dark, but there were a few shimmering objects above her, then she realised she had been banished to the sky, she laughed and said, 'The sky's not much of a punishment. I will find someone to be my slave.'

After a month, Claudia realised there was no one there, she was all alone and she would have to do things for herself. Every time she tried to make herself a meal she got angry, all the anger built up inside her. Then one day, *boom!* Claudia exploded and all her anger and steam escaped from her and floated away and just sat there in the sky.

Zeus called the balls of anger and steam 'clouds' because it sounded a bit like Claudia. Ishmail was then free and lived a very happy life.

Emma Wilkinson (13)
Lodge Park Technology College, Corby

The Rain Maker

The sun was shining, the bees were buzzing and up in the clouds was Ravis, relaxing, sitting on a cloud, soaking up the sun. Suddenly the Earth shook. Ravis woke up and listened. Along came Zais, the leader of the Gods.

'As long as I'm the ruler of this land, there will be no sun! We will live in darkness!' demanded Zais.

Zais then rode up to the sun in fury, with his hands he then shrank the sun with all his power, picked it up and placed it in his pocket.

The flowers drooped, everywhere was in darkness! Ravis loved the sun.

Ravis stood on her cloud and started to cry, she cried so much that her tears ran through the clouds and onto the Earth below. Ravis stood there day after day crying, no one could stop her. Zais rode up to her on his horse and carriage, demanding that she should stop crying. Ravis wouldn't stop, she cried even harder.

'You must stop because it's flooding the land below! If you stop now, I'll bring back the sun!'

Ravis stopped crying, Zais pulled the sun out of his pocket and chucked it back up in the sky, where it became bigger again. Ravis was happy!

'Thank you Zais,' exclaimed Ravis. So the sun shone for thousands of years.

However, whenever Ravis is unhappy, it will always rain.

Stacey Norman (13)
Lodge Park Technology College, Corby

The Creators Of Heaven And Hell

One day Philimena was walking along the shore. Her golden hair was swaying in the wind, her blue eyes twinkling from the sun and her smile as big as always, until she found something. Philimena had found a little baby lying on the shore. It had no clothes on and was only kept warm by the heat of the sun and the sand which acted like a warm blanket on his tiny back.

She picked him up, looked around to see if anyone was looking for their child but no one was in sight, so she decided to keep him.

Philimena was a kind, warm-hearted person who loved everyone and everything. She made pretty blue clothes for her baby to keep warm and she called him Mikalico, as she loved that name. Mikalico had a good, understanding mum and whenever he was in trouble she would help him out. He got everything he needed and he was kind, polite and he was a lovely person to talk to.

When Mikalico was old enough and mature enough, Philimena decided it was best to tell him that she wasn't his real mother. Mikalico seemed okay with that and it made his feelings stronger for Philimena.

That night Mikalico changed, he was angry with Philimena for taking him in. He thought that if she'd left him where he was his parents would've found him but she spoilt his chance. He was going to kill Philimena for looking after him and then kill himself afterwards. He wanted to make an evil place in the afterlife and send people back to Earth to be evil and make others evil because he wanted to be noticed, be a god for some people, be loved.

He told Philimena what his plan was and then killed her. Mikalico didn't know that she was going to do the same but try to keep the world good not evil.

He changed his name to Devillia and called his afterworld Hell and all he had to do now was to kill himself.

The people that were good went to Heaven and the people that were bad went to Hell. They would get taught to be evil or good then sent back to Earth to teach others.

There was one problem though, the people that got sent back to Earth from Hell weren't evil because they didn't want to be tortured again.

Kimberley Johnson (13)
Lodge Park Technology College, Corby

Penelope The Painter

A long time ago, in a land far away, lived a goddess and her daughter. This land was full of joy and colour. Atlanta was the goddess of colour.

Her daughter, Penelope, was sitting quietly as her mother used her mystical paintbrush to paint the world.

Atlanta said to her daughter, 'One day darling, this mystical paintbrush will be yours. You will have a responsible role as the painter of the world.'

Weeks later Atlanta caught an incurable disease and died. Penelope sobbed and sobbed, her mother had always been very close to her, without her mother there was no joy in her. Now that Atlanta had died, the responsibility of bringing colour and joy to the world was down to Penelope.

Penelope was far too sad to paint the world. Slowly the beautiful colours of the world were starting to fade.

Zeus, the most powerful god of all, noticed this and sent his messenger down to tell Penelope to do something about it. Everyone was complaining.

Penelope finally got over her issues, she realised the important role she played. She thought to herself, if her mother was still here, she would be very disappointed.

A few months later, Penelope met a handsome god called Apollo. He was the god of the sun, poetry and music. Apollo charmed Penelope with his wonderful music and poetry. He brought joy back into her life.

For years Penelope carried on this role of painting the world. That's why today we still have these beautiful colours.

Sandy Ngo (13)
Lodge Park Technology College, Corby

Pluto's Daughter

Aphrodite's green hair stood opened around her porcelain face. Her blue eyes were a roar of flame and her porcelain, rosy cheeks were growing redder by the minute. She was furious, humiliated. The goddess of love laughed at by the god of the underworld, Pluto, Aphrodite was not amused.

Staring out from Baydon Hill watching all the beauty of the world Aphrodite would not be calmed, which for the goddess of love was strange. How dare he laugh at her? She wouldn't leave Pluto alone, she would get him back after all, she was much more important.

She walked the Baydon gardens until she found what she was looking for. Pandora, the daughter of Pluto, Aphrodite smirked. Pandora was like her father in many ways - foolish, idle, mischievous but more so like her mother Persephone, when it came to her appearance - Pandora was beautiful.

Aphrodite knew she'd be there somewhere for that was all Pandora was good for, picking the prettiest flowers but nevertheless Pandora was Aphrodite's passage to Pluto.

The bottle of red liquid that Aphrodite handed over was spiked and poisoned, it was clearly just by looking at it but still Pandora, none the wiser, drank it happily. Aphrodite told a dizzy Pandora she looked unwell and should go home to her father.

As Pluto went to hug his daughter, she turned when he spoke, she did not reply. It hurt Pluto deeply, Aphrodite smirked and gloated as she peered down on him.

Aphrodite was so wrapped up in hurting Pluto, everywhere were broken hearts and to this day, a heart is a fragile thing, easily broken.

Sophie Mutch (13)
Lodge Park Technology College, Corby

How Colours Were Made

Three thousand years ago, on a warm and sunny day, Titanious, one of the biggest but not by far, the most popular of the gods, was riding along in his chariot with his bag of paints. Titanious was taking the paints over to an ancient artist in Greece.

He was coming down for landing when his hand slipped off the brake and knocked all of the paints off, spilling them. The artist heard this and came out angrily, he sent Titanious to the head of the gods, Zeus.

When he arrived Zeus was fuming with rage, he sent Titanious out for one hundred days and one hundred nights, to paint the rest of the world.

When Titanious returned, Zeus greeted him and told him, 'Every now and then when the sun is shining, the rain has fallen and the air is clean, I want you to go out and paint the skies with every colour you have, I shall call this a rainbow,' said Zeus.

'OK,' said Titanious.

Titanious still comes out today to paint the skies on the rare occurrence but not to be seen by the eye of man, but to be watched by the microscopic eye of the gods. This is the story of how the world was enchanted with colour.

Jason Claridge (12)
Lodge Park Technology College, Corby

Daphnia And The Seas!

A very long time ago, two people fell madly in love. Those two people were Philodetes and Daphnie. Daphnie was a beautiful young lady, long golden hair, fair skin and a smile no one could resist. Philodetes, on the other hand, was the complete opposite. He had brown hair and was very ugly.

They were both very powerful. Daphnie was the goddess of water and Philodetes was the god of fire.

Daphnie and Philodetes got married and moved into a huge golden castle, surrounded by hundreds of flowers, palm trees and small animals.

For many years, they lived happily married with their daughter, Lucia.

When Lucia was twelve years old, Daphnie saw something strange in a dream. Philodetes was with another woman. She decided to ask Philodetes if he was with another woman but when she did, he shouted at her saying, 'How could you think that? I am your faithful husband.' She decided to leave it at that. Soon she saw the dream again. Philodetes with another woman! This time she decided to find out the truth.

When Lucia was at her friend's, Daphnie told Philodetes she was going out, so when he went out she followed him for many hours, she sat there watching him and her own sister together.

She ran home waiting for him to walk through the doors. When he did, she shouted at him until she could not shout anymore. He knew he had been caught. He left her for a while until she forgave him.

Daphnie cried and cried for days, soon water was building up in the ground. Then rivers and seas were beginning to form until there was no more tears left inside her.

She never got back together with Philodetes. She and Lucia went and lived in a golden castle, and Philodetes lived on an island with no one around him. Daphnie and Lucia lived happily ever after.

Aimee Marchant (13)
Lodge Park Technology College, Corby

How The Clouds Were Made

It was a warm, sunny day in Athens. Medea, the caring and loving mother of Dictys, her imaginative son, was planting some pink roses and Dictys was happily drawing a picture with charcoal, when a huge gust of wind came across them.

Dictys and Medea ran inside, where they carried on drawing and colouring, and then, once the wind had settled, Medea went back outside to finish planting her roses.

Dictys decided it was time for a walk in the woods, Medea allowed him to go, but after a few hours too long, Medea knew something was wrong. Claudiess, the messenger came to tell Medea some bad news.

'Dictys has been hit by a cut down tree, and was dead within minutes of the accident,' said Claudiess, with sorrow.

Medea wept for a long time but then she found the picture that Dictys had drawn earlier that day. Medea raced up to Mount Olympus, where she ordered for clouds to be formed in memory of her dear son Dictys, who was kind to everyone.

Medea ordered Zeus, the head of gods, to form clouds all over the world, in rich and poor parts, in hatred and friendly parts to remember her son, Dictys.

Zeus did as ordered, as he too knew Dictys very well, and so clouds were formed for sun and rain.

Sarah Callan (13)
Lodge Park Technology College, Corby

How The Sun Came To Be . . .

At the beginning of time there was a land full of giants. There were two giants playing hammerball in some fields. The two giants were called Howker and Sutcliff.

Howker and Sutcliff were very strong giants and always won hammerball; together in the summer.

One day while the two giants were playing, Zephaniah, another powerful giant, came and made a proposition to the giants.

Zephaniah asked Howker and Sutcliff if they would play 'fire' hammberball. The two giants talked and thought that they could beat Zephaniah.

Zephaniah only had one 'but'. He would get all their power and gold if he won and they would get all his power and money if they won. The giant's agreed and the date was set to the third day of the new week.

Howker and Sutcliff practised right up to the day of the game. It was the morning of the third day of the new week and the three giants met up. Other giants came to watch.

Zephaniah had the first shot he reached into the neighbouring town. It was time for Sutcliff to have his go and reached into three towns away.

Next, it was Howker's turn. He put his fireball in his chains. He spun around so fast, when he let go the fireball flew up into the sky.

All the giants who were watching gasped at this thing in the sky. It brought light to the Earth - the sun!

Howker and Sutcliff halved Zephaniah's power and gold. They went home happy giants.

Claire Holmes (12)
Lodge Park Technology College, Corby

How We Got Night

Helen, a town's woman, was taking a walk in the woods when a young man in his mid-twenties jumped up behind her and took Helen to his house. All the townspeople saw what was happening but they didn't do anything to stop it.

Up in Heaven, a woman named Bell was spying on Helen, the god, Zeus, was her uncle. She saw what was happening and told Zeus, he was outraged and captured the man. Zeus took him into a room and asked him questions but the man refused to answer the questions apart from one. Zeus asked him what his name was and the man replied Jason.

Jason was taken to an empty room and was to be killed the next day.

That day Zeus was looking down on Earth when there was a knock on the door, it was none other than Helen. A few minutes later Helen walked out with a grin on her face.

As everyone was going to sleep, the Earth went silent, not even a whisper of the wind could be heard.

Zeus awoke to the sound of the townspeople chattering and shopping. Zeus got up and got dressed, putting on his white outfit. Jason was still in the empty room, it was dark without a window and there was not even a bed for Jason to sleep on.

The time had come, Jason was taken to the town and was made to stand there. Nobody knew what was about to happen now, Zeus made an appearance and had changed his mind on the punishment. Instead of killing Jason, he was going to punish the town. Helen had told Zeus what had happened. Now the townspeople watched as she got dragged away.

Zeus put a curse on the town, he said the words, they were such bad words, the townspeople screamed and gasped. Zeus had made darkness afternoon. Darkness would fall upon the people - that meant no shopping.

That's how it is darker in the afternoon but Zeus has forgiven us a bit so night-time falls later.

Tina Madden (13)
Lodge Park Technology College, Corby

Pluto And The Sun

Pluto was king of the Underworld, he was always sad, he wore black and he had silver hair. He was always in the dark.

Every day he would look out onto the world. People were always happy on Earth. The sun shone all the time, it never darkened. Pluto was upset. He wanted people to know what it felt like to live without the sun.

So one day, while Atlas was asleep, Pluto drove up into the sky. There he covered the sun. Afterwards he went back into the Underworld.

Atlas was queen of the sky. She woke to find darkness cast upon the town of Dyer. She could see people were very upset. There was no happiness, people wanted the sun back. Atlas asked the people who had covered the sun. The people of Dyer all shouted out, 'Pluto'. With this, Atlas flew down to the Underworld.

Pluto was sitting in a chair, he was watching the people of Dyer. 'Remove the cover from the sun. The people of Dyer are so unhappy, they are becoming very ill, without the sun,' asked Atlas.

'No, I won't remove the cover, people now know what it is like to live in the dark. I am enjoying it,' laughed Pluto.

'We shall take it to Zeus then,' said Atlas.

They both got into Pluto's chariot and drove up to Olympus. There Zeus sat watching over the Earth.

'What are you two doing here?' asked Zeus.

'I would like Pluto to uncover the sun, but he won't,' replied Atlas.

'I don't want to, it is fun,' giggled Pluto.

Zeus made Atlas and Pluto agree on the matter, he made them agree that the sun would stay covered for another day. If people fell asleep then the sun would be covered for half the day. The other half of day the sun would be uncovered.

So Atlas went back up in the sky and Pluto went down into the Underworld. Both of them sat watching. Atlas didn't want anyone to fall asleep. On the other hand Pluto did. Atlas was upset when people started to fall asleep.

Zeus then told both of them that the dark half of the day, would be called 'night'. The other half would be called 'day'.

At night people had to sleep. During the day they could get up and go about their chores and tasks. That is how we now have day and night.

Amy Cameron (13)
Lodge Park Technology College, Corby

How The Seasons Came To Be

On the Greek islands there were no seasons. It was rarely cold and the wildlife was happy. Penelope controlled the weather and the plants. Her daughter Daphne loved running through the forest and picking berries.

One day when she was in the forest she started singing. Apollo, the sun god, was up on his cloud when he heard her sweet voice, he looked over his cloud and immediately fell in love.

While Daphne was singing, Apollo started playing a harp, Daphne ran to the lake and sat there staring into nothing until her mother Penelope came and told her to go home.

Apollo was heartbroken, but as the sun began to set, he thought of a plan to keep Daphne for himself.

The next day Daphne returned to the lake and bumped into Apollo. He told her he loved her and that he wanted to show her his palace. Daphne refused and started to turn around. Apollo grabbed her, she screamed and struggled. The lake heard this and flowed to the bank to find Penelope.

Apollo returned to the palace with Daphne, he laid her down, by this time, she was too tired to move.

Penelope ran through the forest shouting for Daphne, rain was pouring down, the lake stopped and shouted in a watery voice, 'Apollo has her.'

Penelope ran to the top of Mount Olympus and called for Zeus, she told him what had happened and to get someone up there, Zeus sent Hermes up to the palace.

Daphne had woken up to see Apollo laying out twelve pieces of gold jewellery. Her eyes twinkled. Apollo gave her six pieces to wear. She put them on and admired them.

Hermes came in and told her she could come home if she hadn't worn anything in the palace. Daphne stood there mortified. Her eyes stung with tears.

Hermes returned to Zeus and told him the bad news. Zeus said she had tried on six pieces of jewellery, so he made a deal. For six months Daphne could live with Apollo and the other six months she could be with Penelope.

So when Daphne is with her mother the sun beams and Penelope is happy but when Daphne is with Apollo, Penelope is sad and snow and rain fall and that is how the seasons came to be.

Katie Collins (12)
Lodge Park Technology College, Corby

The Loch Ness Monster

350 million years ago, on an island that would today be known as Australia, there lived a family of dinosaurs, they were called Diplodocus and one of them was called Nessie.

One day when Nessie went hunting with his brothers and sisters he began to feel weak, he felt so weak he couldn't move and eventually couldn't stand, in fact he was so weak it was almost as if his once great legs had turned to fins.

Hours, days, months and years went by and still poor Nessie couldn't walk, for a year he sat under a palm tree wishing he could walk until one day when one of his neighbours' eggs rolled out of the nest, he started crawling to retrieve it, once he realised this, he crawled to the beach to have a drink.

When he reached the beach, he couldn't believe what lay before him. There were thousands of dinosaurs starving, all the vegetation had died away and all that was left was the fish in the sea. Nessie knew he had to do something so he crawled out into the sea and started swimming, caught the fish and brought them back to shore but that wasn't enough, so he swam out to sea.

For years he roamed the world searching for food when he came to the icy water of the North Sea where he'd seen some salmon heading for an island, he followed them over the waterfalls, through rivers and eventually into a great lake.

He had to dive to catch the fish, so he dived to get them when suddenly the water trembled and he could hear an explosion, it was almost like a comet.

He hid under a rock for 350 million years hearing voices above him.

He pops up once in a while to see strange creatures in funny skirts, there he stays wishing to return to his family.

Craig Inglis (13)
Lodge Park Technology College, Corby

The Creature From The Cave

There was once a creature that was hated by all, hated so much that people called him Ity! Ity lived in a cave a few miles away from the town of Beach Island.

It was a sunny day like always. Ity decided to go into the town. Daisy, Princess of Beach Island, was picking flowers in her colourful garden. Ity thought she was beautiful. He wanted to say hello but as soon as he stepped into the garden, a tall young Prince stepped out of his castle. Ity's eyes filled with tears as he watched Prince Jon kiss Daisy. He went back to his dark cave and he realised he had fallen in love with the Princess.

The next day Ity went back to the town determined to get to know Daisy. He found her sitting in her garden he went over to her and they talked for hours. They became good friends.

Daisy realised that she had fallen in love with Ity. She didn't know what to do. She was supposed to be marrying Jon.

She sadly went up to Jon and told him that she had fallen in love with Ity! Jon screamed in rage and stormed out with fury in his eyes.

He went to Ity's cave and got his sword ready. As Ity opened his cave Jon stabbed him in his heart. Jon stepped back as Ity fell to the floor. Daisy ran into his cave and kissed him goodbye. Ity smiled and closed his eyes! Daisy burst into tears.

Jon ran into the hills, never to be seen again!

Rebecca Gill (13)
Lodge Park Technology College, Corby

The Rainbow That Never Ended

Courts, the goddess of hail, was having a nice, calm day when all of a sudden, she heard a loud bang. She got really angry because she knew at once what the terrible noise was.

It was Lulu, the goddess of thunder and lightning. Lulu had just had an argument with her brother, Aries, because he wouldn't help her do anything she asked, so she got really angry and started thunder and lightning.

Cuddlez heard the terrible noises and started getting a bit worried. She thought that the people on Earth might get hurt, so she quickly made it snow and then tried to calm Lulu down by putting snow all over her.

After Lulu had calmed down, Courts decided to make it hail. Aries thought it would be funny to make it rain and full of light, over everything so that made a rainbow and everyone stood staring at the sky because the rainbow was so bright and colourful.

And so it is that ever since Lulu and Aries had that argument there is a rainbow three days a week but it gets brighter each time it happens.

Stephanie Drew (13)
Lodge Park Technology College, Corby

Superstitinus And The Black Cats

There once was a monster called Destructive. This monster was the most blood-curdling terror Ancient Greece had, more than the Minotaur and uglier than the Gorgans. Unlike all other monsters, he had a purpose to kill. Every time a person saw a black cat they would be killed by Destructive. Destructive was a huge, fat cat with long, sharp claws and a face like no other in the world.

There was a young man, Superstitinus, who was walking with his sweetheart, Persephone. They were walking down Marter Street when Persephone saw a black cat. Superstitinus knew she would die and so set off to kill the wretched Destructive once and for all. He knew finding and killing the beast would be hard and dangerous.

He travelled to the island Demitrus where the beast lived. On the way he met Cupid. Cupid was amazed by the love for Persephone so he lent Superstitinus his bow and arrow.

Later when he'd finally arrived in the cave of the beast he awoke the despicable beast.

'You dare enter my domain?' And with saying this the beast lunged at Superstitinus with his eight-inch claws.

Superstitinus acted fast, he grabbed an arrow and stabbed Destructive in the heart, or at least where the heart should have been, for this creature had no heart. That is why the arrow did not fill him with love but kill him. He knew Persephone was now safe.

Now Persephone and Superstitinus are together till death parts them.

This is how the story ends and how the superstition came about that if you see a black cat cross the road, you'll have bad luck.

Daniel Ritchie (12)
Lodge Park Technology College, Corby

Radioactive Freddy

Frederick was exhausted. He had just worked a twelve hour shift at the Jet Bar in London and was on the way to pick up his flatmate Johnny. Johnny worked in a club in town. They both had the following day off and had decided they would try to do more cultural things in future. For the first time since they were kids they were going to go to the Science Museum.

At the Museum Frederick and Johnny were wandering around looking at the dinosaurs. They decided to go and look at the nuclear weapon's display for a laugh. They had arranged to meet their friends Bill, Ted and Roger there. When they arrived the five friends began to muck around, throwing paper at each other and one of the bits of paper hit the radioactive liquid. The radioactive liquid splashed up and hit Frederick. He turned a glowing green colour. The others were scared but Frederick quickly turned back to a normal colour.

Later that evening the five friends went to the club where Johnny worked. A man knocked the table and the drink went all over Frederick. Frederick got cross and went green and everyone ran out of the club. Frederick started to smash the club up and the others tried to calm him down. After about five minutes he calmed down and went back to his normal colour. They all stood there shocked. Frederick didn't remember what had happened.

They went back to the Science Museum and got in through the back door. They went to the nuclear weapon display to try and find a way to stop the same things happening again. They saw a man by the nuclear weapons and asked his name. His name was Professor Atom. The friends explained what had happened and Professor Atom said he could help. He made a potion containing radioactive liquid and kryptonite. He gave it to Frederick to drink.

After Frederick had drank the potion the friends tried to make him angry. They were calling him names, taking the mickey out of him and throwing things at him. Frederick got angry but did not go green and destroy things.

Everyone realised that he had been cured and they were all very happy.

Joshua Campbell (14)
Oak Bank School, Leighton Buzzard

The Minotaur

Firstly I feel you ought to know, Minos is not my real father. My father is a bull and I never get to see him. Also the whole seven youths, seven maidens thing was not my fault; it was my 'stepfather's' idea (as you probably guessed). Another one of my stepfather's ideas was the labyrinth; he told me, 'You'll be out of there before you can say Poseidon'. Do you know how long I have been stuck here? Fifteen years! So it's understandable I have some behavioural difficulties.

It's all I'm remembered as though. A blood-thirsty monster with nothing better to do than eat your children or something. I have feelings too, and that hurts. It gets really lonely here and whenever the youths or maidens, see me they all run away. So I have no friends, I never see my family and 'heroes' keep coming in here trying to slay me! Like, there's some guy in here right now. Calls himself 'Theseus' and he looks so daft clutching his ball of string, wandering around and mumbling to himself. It's so funny when he's on the other side of the wall. I do a tiny growl and he jumps right out of his skin. It's a picture! Not that I'm too afraid. Usually they all starve before they manage to find me.

I think I'll have some fun with this one. I'll jump out and really scare him! He's probably far too weak now to even pack a punch!

Lee-Anne Pawley (14)
St Bernard's RC High School for Girls, Westcliff-on-Sea

The Essence Within

The innocents inside all children pray for the warm sun on their backs, the lukewarm rays beautifully caressing their soft, supple cheeks, the smell of the fresh cut grass blown to them by the friendly cooling breeze of summer. But no, not us, we pray for thunder, thunder and thrashing rain beating against the shattering windows, anything, anything to drown out the roars of 'the' raging parents.

Looking up at the sodden wall towering over me I lay in the stillness of the night, you whisper to me, 'Goodnight sweet dreams,' and close the plank of a door but don't get far enough. Immediately you hiss at each other, thinking I'm deaf, 'Don't you understand what you're doing to me?'

The marks on the wall go deeper than the ocean, the darkening colour of the wall camouflage with the rock carrying bags under my eyes, like the marks do my skin. The endless times those fists have accidentally collided with my face is too many to count.

The splintered mirror stands before me, casting an unfriendly shadow across my darkening features. The single tear staggers down my cratered face, as I wait for the end. When the fierce emotions collide with my frail body for the last time. Ending all torture, and banishing light from my 'life' forever. The wind is crashing and the rain is shattering, but there's no shouting, and so this is the beginning for me again, another night or will it finally be the end?

Rosie Underhill (13)
St Bernard's RC High School for Girls, Westcliff-on-Sea

A Day In The Life Of A Factory Worker

Looking back on it now from up above, I feel deprived of a first love, a first kiss, a first child of my own, deprived of a lifetime.

I awoke before the sun had stretched his long golden fingers over our once beautiful land now disrupted by famine and war. I thought of the dream that had left a smile on my face and an imprint on my heart, a dream of my childhood, five short years of playing in the road without a care. I stared at my hands worked to shreds by the loom, it's funny the loom was my lifeline, but would one day be my cause of death. I stared at my sore stomach bloated from lack of food. I stared at my legs, whipped, bruised and as thin as my father's patience.

I stared at the factory surrounding me, it was my home, my school and my church. I saw my friends, their crisp, warm tears slide down their cheek like lies from a sinner's tongue onto the floor that was their bed.

The day passed in a blurred greyness as all the windows were boarded up, we did not know when the day ended but I had a piece that needed finishing for the very next sunrise and so carried on. I was alone in the factory all those around me were asleep beneath their looms, how I wanted to sleep just for a second. How I wanted to dream just . . . for . . . a . . .

Alice Nutman (12)
St Bernard's RC High School for Girls, Westcliff-on-Sea

My Vortex Nightmare

I'm so angry with my mum; I mean staying up till ten is going to make a big difference. So here I am outside of my local forest, kicking the dirt. I've got an idea! What if I went in the forest and ran away! Yes! I'll run away . . .

In I tiptoed so quietly, reacting to every movement around. Jumping and turning, not missing a thing. The crunch of the leaves beneath my feet, the cool, whistling of the wind, blowing my hair into my face, blocking all sight, leading me into a vortex of nightmares. The leaves and wind were working together forming some sort of system, the wind picking up the leaves and swirling me down, down into the depths of the piles of leaves. I found myself moving deeper and deeper into the midst of the forest. I was losing control, becoming insane with the thought of the crunch of the leaves and swirl of the wind. The forest was drawing, sucking me in.

I'm lost. The crunching and swirling had died down. The silence was becoming tense. Out of the corner of my eye I spotted the trees. I became anxious. Their branches were like hands scratching and smothering me. The leaves were like wild bushy hair swaying from side to side. The carvings in the wood show a face: angry, sharp eyes, a mouth with pointy, blood-hungry teeth and eyebrows raised so high. What was I to do? Would I ever get out of this hungry vortex?

Emma Marie Lynch (12)
St Bernard's RC High School for Girls, Westcliff-on-Sea

A Mother's Love

I was frozen to the spot, colour draining out of my face. The smell of the forest reminded me of something, my darling nan. If only I could just reach out and kiss her, hug her, tell her I need her by my side for the rest of my life . . . but . . . she's not here. The smell of death and blood lingered in the air.

Anger was boiling up inside me. I turned round and got a good look at my parents, the people I should love. I don't love them, I detest them and every minute of the day I wish they were dead, out of my life forever. The sight of them made me feel like vomiting, I turned back; all I could see was trees surrounding me closing in on me, waiting to hear the death cry . . . of me.

I have no real mother, but I have a grandma. And I believe if I die this minute she'll be there. She will clench me so tight and tell me that phrase that every child in the universe has heard except me 'I love you'. To be loved is harder than winning the lottery, not for everyone, just me.

I turned, they had gone, I looked into the sky, three white doves flew past and dropped three white tulips. Suddenly a sharp dagger flew towards me, breaking my heart, reuniting my soul with my grandma, for the first time in my life I'm happy, in Heaven for evermore.

Chantelle Ryan (13)
St Bernard's RC High School for Girls, Westcliff-on-Sea

The Figure In The Woods!

There I was walking into the dark woods all on my own, with lots of layers on. It was a cold, bitter night and the chilly breeze was biting into my coat. It was misty and foggy so I couldn't really see where I was going. I was being very curious of where I was putting my feet and it was very muddy. I thought I could see a figure in front of me but I couldn't quite see. He looked scary and had ragged clothes on. He was wearing a hat and big black army boots. He was coming closer and closer towards me, I didn't know what to do or say. I stood there still as a rock, not knowing where I was or what to do, run or stay right where I was. I saw his eyes. They were bright blue with big pupils. I started to move back.

I took one big step and a deep breath. I heard him say something, something like, 'Don't move, stay right where you are or else!' By this time I was really scared and again didn't know what to do.

The trees started to groan and fall into me, the leaves were crunching underneath my feet.

Then suddenly I felt a hand cover my mouth and I started to be dragged away. I was screaming and screaming . . .

Rhiannon Thomas (13)
St Bernard's RC High School for Girls, Westcliff-on-Sea

Dream Or Reality?

A young girl laid awkwardly on rough ground, her thick black hair streaked with dirt, trees completely surrounding her, tiny glints of sunlight reflecting off her porcelain skin. Her family stood solemnly around her, they stood as if in a daze staring at her pure white nightgown speckled with dirt like the colour of the moon on a cloudy night, her ruby-red lips set in a frown and her thin black eyebrows set in a look of pure bedazzlement.

The wind gently whispered around her rustling the leaves. As if a wake up call the young girl gently lifted her head rubbing the sleep out of her eyes. She stared at her family, her eyes full of confusion. 'Mum, Dad what's going on?'

'We are here to say goodbye.' Her parents' faces were full of sorrow and dread. They no longer looked real as the young girl had once seen them. Their dark shadows swamped her.

They clenched each other's hands tightly, tears trickling down their faces. One by one the tears hit the ground echoing through the young girl's ears. The sound became louder and louder, the young girl begged them to stop. Suddenly pain from their sorrow hit her throwing her onto the floor drilling through her mind, her parents stared on.

It was early morning and a young girl's mum walked into her child's bedroom, she could not breathe or cry about the sight before her.

Shelby Ryan (13)
St Bernard's RC High School for Girls, Westcliff-on-Sea

An Evacuee

I never thought it would come to this! Not up until Mum told me I had to go away. She said it was a holiday, but I knew it wouldn't be fun. It started when I was sitting on the train saying goodbye, Mum was crying, but I felt numb. I don't think I quite got over the shock. Even today I still think of Mum's face as the train pulled away.

It was about 2 o'clock when I arrived at Maggie's. I was scared! I knocked only to find a young woman open the door and invite me in. It carried on when I arrived at my room to discover two other girls my age there, scared and lonely, like me.

That night I didn't sleep well, I kept thinking of Mum back in our house, waiting for a siren to sound so she could get to the bomb shelter. I am so scared for both our lives. Why did it lead to this? *War!* I hate it!

I woke at 4am next morning, scared, as Dad died a few weeks ago, I didn't want to lose Mum as well.

The day after wasn't so bad as I spoke to Leanne, one of the girls in my room, she said she'd been here a couple of weeks now and that she is used to it here.

It's been two months for me but I still want to go home, to my own house.

Marie Goldsworthy (13)
St Bernard's RC High School for Girls, Westcliff-on-Sea

Prison Of Haunts

Here it is, the outspoken, blood-curdling group of Haunts. I look up, slowly scanning the entrance to the fearsome prison of expectant, alarming creatures. Here I go, the step, life or death, this is the moment, I enter with all my courage and determination.

I see the depth of the forbidden earth beneath my feet, the trees clouding over me. The bushes rustle, they hint something isn't right. I freeze, leaves scatter and wind whistles.

I edge nearer to what I believe is a mysterious world. I breathe heavier, an unnatural light flickers through the trees. Butterflies hover, birds sing, a whole new world develops around me. My mouth is gorged open, not a word or breath could travel into this third dimension.

I close and open my eyes, this was beyond my imagination, not a thought, or a hard studied idea could live up to this mind-blowing situation. In the distance, I see something, it's moving.

I carry on through the butterflies, it's unimaginable, I look harder and harder. The sky turns turquoise, it gets darker. I blink, the unnatural light vanishes. The colourful creatures disappear. The clouds go dark, they flash. I blink.

Here I am, the eerie woods back to normal, what about all the optimistic things? The trees creak. Fog covers what was a loveable sky. It forms an unmissable silhouette. I run. Twigs creak. Stones ping. Never again will I go near the Prison of Haunts.

Sophie Lark (13)
St Bernard's RC High School for Girls, Westcliff-on-Sea

Short Story

Dear Mum and Dad,

Today I have hardly done anything. I have played with my friend Lucy. She is a really nice friend. I do also play with Claire and Peter as they only have one or two friends. I am so bored and I really miss you. It's just not right without you both. I hate my foster carers. They don't like me at all. I wish they would . . .

Anyway, I really miss you. I think of you day and night. In my bed I think of you, then start to cry and don't stop 'til I fall asleep. Claire and Peter always end up sleeping with me. They always cry, at least twice a day.

Let's talk about Lucy. She is very nice. She has got a brother and sister as well, like me. Her dad is in the war and her mum is working. You might know her actually. She is called Jayne Milcock. Do you know her?

Claire said that she really misses you. She has made a friend called Sophie. She is the age of Claire. Peter said he has made two friends, Stephen and Sam. They are really nice and their mum and dad are in the war.

We really miss you, can't we come home? I know what, you could come over here and we could all live somewhere around here. It is so boring here. The food, well it is horrible and we hardly get anything.

We miss you.

Love from Lucy.

Sarah Rimmington (12)
St Bernard's RC High School for Girls, Westcliff-on-Sea

Screaming Dolly!

Things haven't been quite right since my mum's new boyfriend 'Jack' moved in. He thinks I'm a baby! He buys me dolls and Barbies! I'm fourteen! I told Mum, but she thinks I'm just jealous. He's loaded down with toys every day! He says I need to live a more enjoyable life. I spoke to my best friend Nicky and she suggests that I should start a diary for my thoughts and secrets, so I decided to walk her way . . . !

10/9/06

Today I went down to the basement to put more toys in! It was really dark and gloomy! The door slammed behind me. I couldn't get out! The darkness was reaching out to get me. It stared at me. I stared back! It grew fingers and nails! That's when it started scratching my arms and legs! It was patterned like a quilt. The basement was spinning round and round around me!

I then heard a sudden noise. A 'screech'! I followed the noise to see what it was. My heart beat really fast! I felt something touch me. It felt like a small hand. But I thought to myself, *nonsense!* I continued walking. She jumped out right in front of me! It was a doll! She screamed at me! It deafened me. I shouted for help, but no one came! I thought this was the end and indeed it was!

My bones lay here scattered until someone finds them, so for the conclusion of this story/diary . . . I'm just a ghost!

Michelle Regnaud-Carvalho (11)
St Bernard's RC High School for Girls, Westcliff-on-Sea

It Was Only A Dare . . .

It was only a dare. A stupid dare. I could have backed out, but I was too proud. I wanted to earn the respect of my friends, but lying here in this hospital makes it seem so worthless now. I thought it wouldn't hurt me. I was wrong.

We were bored, so we went to the lake. A dog was barking in a back garden and it kind of got on my nerves. I shouted, 'Shut it, you stupid dog!'

It got louder.

'Let's shut that dog up! I'm as bored here as I was down the town,' shouted Lucie. She got up and we all followed her to the garden where the dog was.

It was a huge dog! I was very scared. I tried to edge away but Lucie saw. She took me by the arm and led me to the door. She opened it.

'I dare you to shut up that dog! Or are you too scared?'

'Fine!'

I went in. It was chained up, so I let out a sigh of relief. I found a toy and put it in the dog's mouth. No noise. I could hear my friends cheering me. I turned to go and I heard a crunch. The chain was broken! I ran for the gate and told them to open it.

'The dog's barking again! You're not coming out until it's quiet!'

It nearly killed me. I hate my mates. And that dog.

Rebecca Miller (12)
St Bernard's RC High School for Girls, Westcliff-on-Sea

A Day In The Life Of My Mum

Oh God, it's Thursday, work today, I'm dreading it! I have to get out of bed now, Jessica's moaning about a sore throat again. Oh no, here goes Tom, 'Mum, I don't want to go to school today, I feel sick. How come Jessica's staying off?'

I have to go through this every morning, that's the problem with having two almost the same age, they fight!

'Mum, I need a drink.' There she goes again. 'Mum, where are my shoes? And I can't find my coat.' And Tom as well, great a perfect start to my day - *not!*

Does every mum go through this? At least one of mine is old enough to look after herself, mind you Joe's not too bad, at least he doesn't make a fuss in the morning!

Oh no, here comes trouble, the first day he's been in all week! That's the thing with being a teacher, whenever you come in the terrors come in with you. Thank God it's break, I can have a rest, I had to plan art for today didn't I, *big* mistake! I'll wait till lunch then I'll tell the head teacher I feel sick and then I'll go home - *woo hoo!*

I'm relaxed now. I'll just go and pick Tom up from school, wait a while, then go and get Jess and Joe from the bus stop - simple. That rest has done me some good.

Time for bed I think; the kids have done their homework and we're ready for tomorrow - I hope!

Jessica Ackland (12)
St Bernard's RC High School for Girls, Westcliff-on-Sea

Ordinary Decent Criminal

I crept down the stairs as quiet as a mouse. Stan once told me, 'Now Johnny Boy whilst you're on a job be quick, quiet and don't get involved.'

Oh sorry, I forgot to introduce myself. I am called Johnny (Johnny Boy to my mates). I'm 24 and I'm a handyman. Not your normal gardening, few jobs around the house man. I'm talking about your thieving handyman. I do little and sometimes big jobs for the proper gangsters. You know getting rid of people, that type of thing.

I'm just off to Tony's bar to meet my brother, Luther, he's a gang leader and he wants me to do a job for him. There he is sitting in the window in his flash Gucci suit. 'Hi, bro,' I said in my deep husky voice. 'What do you need doing?' I questioned him.

'Well you know Malachi Jones? He's been shacking up with Stan's missus. I need you to have a few . . . words with her?'

'OK, I will do, see you later.'

When I was about to walk away he grabbed my arm. 'Don't let me down bro.'

'Whatever,' and I shrugged him off.

So there I was driving to Luther's house watching the kids playing happily and I wished that they'd never grow up. Then I remembered I was driving, I grabbed the steering wheel, turned off the engine and walked to the door.

As soon as I saw Caillie I knew I was in love . . .

Jade-Louise Fort (12)
St Bernard's RC High School for Girls, Westcliff-on-Sea

A Day In The Life Of A . . .

'G'day mates, my name's Jack. I'm a, well, I'm not gonna tell ya that. Ya gonna have to read my story and guess. Alright? Good. Well this is what happened . . .

I was hanging out with my mates under our favourite eucalyptus tree, chewing on a blade of grass, when suddenly, we heard this deafening bang. It was hunters. We knew that it was the hunters; it's just, they're never usually out at this time. We ran for our lives and suddenly, I fell down a hole.

I was knocked out for a few hours; eventually I opened my eyes. I was blinded by the light streaming in from around me. I knew it wasn't home; so, I started to explore. I was confused. It looked the same; but there was something wrong. It was almost spooky. There was no one around. I went into town, to see if my friends were there, but everywhere was empty. All I could hear was the wind whistling behind my ears.

Quietly, I heard a small whisper that grew. 'Jack, Jack,' it called. I opened my eyes, and there in front of me were my mates.

'What happened?' I asked.

'You fell down a hole and believe it or not, you knocked y'self out!'

'Crikey,' I gasped. 'That was a bumpy ride.'

I got up with a hop, skip and a jump and started telling my mates what had happened. It was a weird experience.

Did you guess what I am?

A kangaroo.

Georgia Chapelle (12)
St Bernard's RC High School for Girls, Westcliff-on-Sea

A Day In The Life Of Dan Goodblade

Dan sets out his day as usual. Up at six just like any other 15-year-old boy. Only he's not.

'I woke up at six this morning (stupid milk cart). Found a Gap jumper in the trash and thought, *why me?* So I took it. Very snug. So sorry, I didn't introduce myself. My name is Dan Goodblade. I'm 15. My dad's in the nick, and my mum died when she gave birth to me. Life was never easy. I enjoyed school though. English was my favourite subject.

At home it was a different matter. I don't think he ever really got over Mum's death. We had a laugh every now and again but things could have been better. Anyway, one day we were watching EastEnders and there was a knock at the door. It was the police. Someone had pressed charges on Dad for beating him up (a drunken row). Dad pleaded guilty and got 18 months for GBH, that's why I'm here now. I suppose I could have stayed at home, but I can't pay the mortgage, so I'd have been made homeless anyway. Wish I could have furthered my education though. I wonder if my friends miss me? 'Cause I sure miss them. I'm so bored, and hungry. I've got £2. I think I'll pop into McDonald's.

That burger tasted so good. So did that Coke. I'm tired. It's late, and as for the story of a homeless boy - that's about it.

Melissa Bonnelame (12)
St Bernard's RC High School for Girls, Westcliff-on-Sea

Time

Rachel Daniels raced downstairs, two steps at a time. She needed to get to school! 'Bye Mum!' she gabbled and then she was speeding down the street so quickly that she should have been fined! After running for what seemed like forever, a bell sounded in her ears, far-off in the distance. 'Oh crap!' Rachel shrieked. 'Not again!'

Finally, she arrived at school, miraculously before Mr Hashmal.

'Rachel's late? What a shock!' Rachel's best mate Davey said, grinning.

'Shut up you!' she said, grinning as well.

Sliding into her seat, Rachel began to fiddle with her watch. At the exact second that Mr Hashmal walked in, Rachel pulled out the silver button on her watch. For a moment, she didn't notice anything. Then she began to wonder at the silence all around. What had happened? Slowly, her heart pounding, she looked up. Everybody was still. Not a finger moved, not a sound pierced the air. Rachel's breathing quickened.

After about a minute, she acted out of instinct and pushed the button in again.

Suddenly, life was restored to the room. Mr Hashmal sat down at his desk, a paper aeroplane reached its target. Turning about wildly, she looked at Davey.

'What just happened?' she asked puzzled.

Davey frowned. 'What do you mean?' he asked. (Rachel was weird sometimes!)

'Never mind,' said Rachel, turning away. Was it possible? Rachel wondered. Could her old watch possibly . . .

Suddenly Rachel smiled. She could stop time.

Emma Sampford (12)
St Bernard's RC High School for Girls, Westcliff-on-Sea

The Break Of Dawn

The break of dawn as a tear ran down my face, not from my devastated heart but from the factory that glowed. As my bruised legs carried me along I saw a pound, my legs had enough energy to bend and pick it up, suddenly two older, richer and dejected boys yelled that it was their dirty coin just like their heart.

My hands were coated in black as I threw the coal in the warm, sweating fire. I could see all the children learning to spell, write and read.

As the lunch bell rang my stomach growled like the tiger's stomach just before pounce, it was the same ghastly gruel as every aching day. As I had finished my so-called food I grabbed my shovel and dug the coal. It was pay day and my money seemed to smile, as I gripped it tight it started to turn black from my cut and bony hands.

As I slowly walked to my dump, the sun was slowly setting for it had enough of going up and down and seeing the same boring world. There was a shadowed figure standing, it looked as if I had seen her when my eyes glazed on the world for the first time.

Who . . . ?

Robyn Strauss (11)
St Bernard's RC High School for Girls, Westcliff-on-Sea

A Little Girl's Story

It started out to be a great day, I had done everything except a little bit of homework so I went to the library after school to do it. It was nearly closing time so I rushed to the toilet, when I got back I packed up my things and made my way to the entrance door. Only when I got there it was locked, my happy spirits fell all the way to the floor . . .

But then I remembered the back door! I ran as fast as my legs could take me but it was locked too. So I sat down and tried to be relaxed until I heard a funny noise so I got up and followed the noise, it was strange as it took me to the stock room . . .

As I opened the door something jumped on my face, 'Argh!' *Oh God,* I thought it was a monster but it was only a cat. I was scared but glad as I had company. I looked at my watch, 7.30, I'd missed EastEnders but that was the least of my worries - my parents!

I had nothing left to do except go to sleep so I did.

In the morning a loud bang on the door woke me up, it was my parents and the police at the door! The cat was gone, I was relieved my parents were there but I wanted to look for the cat, everyone helped but we had no luck.

The next week I heard the same thing happened to another girl only she was there all weekend! And *dead!* They say she died from deep cat scratch marks. I thought to myself, *if I wasn't found would I be dead?* I always thought school was a safe place, not now.

Catherine Birch (12)
St Bernard's RC High School for Girls, Westcliff-on-Sea

Devil Dog

It was looking at me, could it be, no of course not, it was like it was always there, never leaving me.

'Argh!'

It got me, a massive chunk out of my arm.

Thank goodness, only a dream, my bed was full of sweat, I had to pop to the bathroom to wipe my face with a flannel. I was finally at the bathroom, looking round every corner making sure there was no one there. 'Ah,' that feels so lovely and cold. Then the problem started. I heard creaks coming up the landing then I saw a shadow. I closed my eyes in so much stress. Then I quickly peeped through my fingers. It was only my little doggy, he seemed very strange, his eyes weren't normal (they are normally green) but his were red. I was wondering if it was my dog, or could it be just a lookalike? The dog was getting his claws out, it looked like it was on a mission to kill me. I screamed, 'Argh!'

Everyone rushed into the bathroom even my brother and sister.

'What in the Devil is going on in here?'

'W-w-e-e-l-l-l . . .'

'Oh dear, just tell me in the morning.'

So I rushed back to my bed and I was asleep as quickly as lightning.

Morning finally came, Mum wasn't there, she had probably gone to fetch the morning paper as she always does on a Saturday morning. I switched on the television till Mum got back. The dog was still asleep, the television was full blast, so the dog had woken up in a shot. It came up on the sofa acting all nice like it loved me, then the red eyes appeared again, the claws came out, I was shivering with fright, then Mum walked through the door with the paper in her hand.

'So what was all this screaming last night?'

The dog quickly jumped off the sofa back onto his bed.

'It was the dog, he was trying to kill me!'

'What, that cute little doggy that's over there?' said Mum.

'Yes,' I shouted.

It had his red eyes back on, I knew exactly what he was thinking, just waiting for my mum to go out of the room, then he would get me . . .

Tiffany Bryan (11)
St Bernard's RC High School for Girls, Westcliff-on-Sea

Young Writers – That's Write! Eastern Counties

A Day In The Life Of Claire Sanders

It's my birthday today. Funny I should be thirty, married, in love and have children. But here I am living with my mum, free and single. I was only ten you know. All I wanted was to be like her. Everyone did. Claire Sanders, coolest girl in school.

Claire had beautiful, long, golden locks, pearly blue eyes, perfect figure and then there's me. I have black, straight, put back in a ponytail hair, green eyes and am just a tad overweight.

It was weird, I prayed on a star that I would be just like her. I woke up and nothing, so that night when I went to bed I forgot to pray. When I woke I thought I had slept over somebody's house. Pink wallpaper, pink, pink everything. Four-poster bed and a mirror. Then when I sat up I thought I was having a great dream, here I was sitting in Claire's bed, Claire's face, hair, body, everything.

I got up, went to school and, well, bumped into me. There was fear in my eyes, cold, awful fear and that's when I realised it was real, I was her and she was me.

It was great. Claire's mates were all around me laughing. I actually felt cool, but every now and then I would see the real me, all alone.

The next day, everything was back to normal, except Claire, coolest girl in school, came to make friends with me.

Rachel Gibson (13)
St Bernard's RC High School for Girls, Westcliff-on-Sea

The Regret

I never really used to work hard.

That was in the evening, when I went to bed.

'Lisa, Lisa,' they called me.

'What now?' I answered hesitantly. I went off and sat on the chair.

'Now what do you think this is, eh?' Dad asked. 'And why are you getting all these nasty grades?' he said. His face showed he was very furious. 'Lisa, I tell you my child, you better work hard, it does not mean you will stay with us forever, time shall come, and all these things shall go.'

'I don't care, as long as I live and enjoy myself,' I said rudely. I couldn't even be bothered to take a book and read.

The next day, Mum had been sick from malaria and was in hospital, until when I was in school I heard she was dead. It was now me and Dad left and I was the only child. Things then got worse, Dad kept on thinking about the death of Mum.

He had not been going to work for three weeks and he was the manager. When he went to work, he was shocked when he heard he was fired, then he was involved in a car accident.

It was a shame really, no will at all and some relatives had come to get most of the things and I never even knew them.

Everything was gone. I was nothing but a stupid person. I cried.

'Lisa, wake up or else you will be late for school, and why are you crying?'

Oh, it was just a dream. Since then I've worked hard in school.

Priscilla Kananji (13)
St Bernard's RC High School for Girls, Westcliff-on-Sea

A Day In The Life Of Britney Murphy

I woke up, the smell of cigarettes hit me. I groaned. I rolled over to check the clock: 12.36! Sugar! I was 2 hours late for my new film. How was I going to explain this? 'Oh sorry I'm late. Just out partying,' or the sensible lie, 'Sorry my alarm didn't go off!'

Finally I got there. Paul Rosenburg wasn't too pleased with me. He ended up wasting another hour lecturing me about time wasters. Yeah right. He can talk.

At around 2 o'clock Marshall finally arrived. Together we had to act out a scene. He had bought his little girl, Hailie-Jade, with him and she was playing with her Barbie. Finally we got to work, sometimes acting seriously, other times forgetting our lines and starting again. It was a very long afternoon.

Finally I got home, it was 10.57 and I still had jobs to do. First I had to have a bath, then I had to walk the dogs, then I had to eat and then I had to arrange a date for an interview with 'Top of the Pops'. *Hopefully* I thought, *there will be no one to answer the phone.* I laughed harshly when the buzzer went to my door.

I opened it and there in the doorway was . . . Paul Rosenburg, with a handful of scripts. I laughed a nervous laugh, so I shut the door, knocking him out.

This is just not my day!

Leanne Elcoate (12)
St Bernard's RC High School for Girls, Westcliff-on-Sea

How The Snake Got Its Bite!

A long time ago in a faraway land, near Eastern Asia was a small village called Mera. The people in that village were not very wealthy and they made their own things, grew their own crops and even built their own houses.

A young boy called Hardoo lived in a small house in the centre of the village.

Every morning Hardoo did his chore, they were to get up early, feed the chickens, and milk the cow. After that Hardoo went with his father to the field. There Hardoo would pick the oranges, mangoes and other fruits that he and his family were going to eat for the day, while his father cut large bundles of grass to keep the field neat for the next time he grew something there.

After a long day's work, Hardoo and his father came home. Hardoo unfortunately had to tie the grass bundles up with the string his mother made from old wheat strands. When he went to fetch the string, he noticed it wouldn't be enough, so he decided to look for something else. Hardoo looked around until he spotted what looked like another piece of string. It was hard to tell because it was the evening and there was no light. Hardoo went up to the long, thin-looking thing and picked it up, suddenly it moved vigorously and hissed. It was a snake! Hardoo had the fright of his life, but he also had an idea, he thought he could use the snake to tie the grass with, and so he did.

Later that evening his father found the grass with the snake around it. Hardoo told him about the idea. Everybody thought it was great, but the snake hated this and prayed for help.

One day while slithering around, a snake found a bottle of thick blue liquid. Suddenly something appeared before it. The thing told the snake it would give all the snakes a poisonous bite if they drank it. The snake, shocked but excited at this drank, it and gave it to every snake it knew.

Not much later, all the snakes had got the poisonous bite.

The villagers soon finding out about this were horrified and left the snakes from then on, thinking they wouldn't interfere with the creatures of God.

Shamreen Bi (13)
St John Fisher RC School, Peterborough

The House On The Hill

It was a cold, quiet, creepy night down in the small town of Tallville. The moon was full and shining brightly, all apart from the house on top of the hill. An old tree arched over the entrance of the house, with the owl sitting as still as a log on top of the branch.

As Toby approached the house that very night, he crept quietly not making a noise. He needed to get his ball back that he had kicked over a few minutes before. He reached for the doorbell, the door creaked open. Toby was not sure what to do. Unconfidently, he walked into the house. The door slammed behind him with a thud. Toby, shaking like a leaf, jumped around in a 180-degree motion. He stepped forward towards the large, spiral staircase. As he did this, he noticed a green light coming out of a door under the stairs that looked as if it led into a basement. He opened his mouth widely as if he was about to shout as loud as he could, instead, a quiet voice came out asking if anyone was there.

He slowly walked towards the basement door. As he came closer the sound of a mumbling man became noticeable. He came to the door frame and asked himself if it was wise to go down. Something inside him was telling him to go down and investigate; he followed this inkling and went down.

Still scared, he crept down, poking his head round a corner. There he saw a man with frizzled hair drinking a green liquid in a flask. The man turned round, saw Toby, and chased after him. Toby ran as fast as he could out of the house and jumped the gate, which the tree bowed over. As the man ran back into the house in his torn shoes, Toby noticed what looked like to be wings on his back. Toby never went anywhere near the house again.

Sam Harwin (13)
St John Fisher RC School, Peterborough

A Day In The Life Of Judy Carrmichael

Judy Carrmichael is a 24-year-old social worker, in a vocational full-time job. Nothing out of the ordinary there. But today is like no other, oh no, today will become a day to remember, as today, Judy Carrmichael will make one of the most important choices a woman will ever make!

Abortion. Today at 3.35pm, Judy will have to go forth with her decision to have an abortion. Now, Judy herself has no knowledge of her real birth mother, as she was adopted, so this decision to put her foetus in the position of death, was a big one. She herself, does not want to go through with it, yet her foster mother Ruth, thinks it is in her best interest to do so.

It is now 3.11pm. Here Judy is in the waiting room, waiting, waiting. Every possible excuse Judy can use is now running through her head. She's thinking about how she felt when she met her foster mother - guilty, nervous, scared, unlucky.

3.33pm. Doctor Mazumba calls her name out. A sudden sharp pain jolts its way up Judy's spine, she can't see, all her senses fade away as she falls and her skull bounces on the floor like Michael Jordan's basketball in training. She's starting to fit. Blank.

'Judy, Judy, Judy.' Ruth is so scared, all she can say is, 'Judy.'

Finally, Judy comes around, so there she is lying on a hospital bed. She can't remember what happened, all she can remember is entering the hospital. That was her last recollection of where she was. Abortion. The doctor's piercing eyes stare at Judy's as she sits up. Judy doesn't know what she's doing at the hospital as she can still feel the baby inside her. Then with a last gasp of breath, she falls back down and falls unconscious. Dead.

Ethan Nash (13)
St John Fisher RC School, Peterborough

A Day In The Life Of A Trainer

I started off in a damp and cold factory with lots and lots of machinery around me. I was getting passed down to each machine by workmen and being thrown around and then attached to different fabrics.

Then me and my friends were put in a big brown box and exported to different countries and then finally delivered to a place people like to call 'the shoe shop'.

Next thing that happened is I was separated from my friends and placed on a nice shelf, where I met new shoes and made new friends! While sitting on my new shelf I wondered if the next person would buy me.

Soon after, the waiting is over and a nice lady walks in and looks at me, and decides she wants to buy me. I am picked up and placed on the cold surface of the counter and then put into a plastic bag with the words 'Shoe Palace' on. Then I am carried to my new home.

When I get to my new house I find a big German shepherd dog waiting for me and I think I will be chewed up, but luckily the dog sleeps most days!

I am taken out of my cupboard and put on at 7pm most nights.

We go to the park and walk the dog. I have so much fun kicking the ball to the dog and he always brings it back to me!

Then we go home and I am cleaned and placed in my cupboard until the next night!

Now I can't wait to take the dog out again!

Leah Hobbs (14)
St John Fisher RC School, Peterborough

A Day In The Life Of . . .

Oh no, it's that time again, there goes the alarm, *beep, beep, beep.* Have you ever heard any noise that is more annoying? Better get moving, no point in just lying here. Breakfast first I think, same old thing every morning, boring. One day I'm going to get myself something really exciting and different to eat but not today because I can't be bothered.

It's raining outside but I have to go out, I don't get a choice, all day in the rain and cold. I hate the rain. I love it when it's really hot and sunny, and I can just lie sunbathing all day long! Here we go, blimey that is cold, glad I have my warm coat on. Let's have a walk around, I have my brother following me today, he's OK sometimes but today I would like to be alone.

Who's that over there? Oh, it's my mate Tommy. 'You alright Tommy? How are you?' He's my best mate, my brother is still following me, he's so embarrassing! I really wish he would go, I just know he's going to say something to show me up! We've ended up in the park.

Look at that bird over there, she's tasty!" I can see Tommy has his eye on her too. She's mine, I saw her first. I look at Tommy and he looks at me then we end up laughing, we aren't going to fall out over a bird, there are plenty more around.

My brother is starting to whine, he doesn't like being so far away from the house. I can tell he's getting on Tommy's nerves.

'Shut him up will you?' Tommy shouts at me.

I hate it when this happens because Tommy is my best mate, but I'm supposed to stick up for my brother aren't I? What shall I do? What shall I do? Here we go, another argument with my best mate because of my stupid, scared brother. 'Don't shout at me,' I reply, 'he can't help it if he's not as brave as me and you.' And with that I grab my brother by the scruff of his neck and run away as fast as I can. Even though Tommy is my best friend he will always win a fight, I wasn't hanging around to let him beat me again.

When we get home it is time to go in, just in time for a quick snooze before tea. Same old boring food again to eat, but I am so hungry I don't care! I ask to go out again before we go to bed and I am allowed. I go to find Tommy and apologise, my little brother isn't with me this time.

I find Tommy and he says it is OK, just that my brother really winds him up sometimes, I agree with him and tell him I'm not allowed to be out late so I have to go.

I go back home, and straight to bed. I've had a long day. No one realises how hard life can be . . . being a cat!

Becky Weston (13)
St John Fisher RC School, Peterborough

A Day In The Life Of A Shoe

Hi, I'm a trainer. I'm not sure what my name is but it appears to say something like N-i- . . . kee . . . on the side of my partner, so I figure that must be my name too. I think I must have been really bad in a past life to be reincarnated as a shoe! People treat me like something they've stood in!

From what I heard of a conversation my owner was having, I think today is football practise. That means he won't be needing me, he owns a shiny new pair of football boots, a nice relaxing day with the missus then! But where are those boots? I haven't seen them on the shoe rack for two days now. I best stop writing for a second I think 'he' is coming . . . what . . . what's going on! Oh no! He's putting us in his boot bag! Tell you what, I'll stop writing for now and let you know what happens tonight.

Huh! I hate football! That's what *football* boots are made for! Now I'm shattered and covered in mud too! I have a splitting headache! Anyway best get some rest, night-night! Snore . . . snore . . .

Hannah Hill (13)
St John Fisher RC School, Peterborough

The Dysfunctional Life

Hi, my name is Aaron and I am 13 years old, but I don't have a very normal childhood.

My family are a bit different from all my friends' families, mine are so bad my mates' parents have banned them from coming round mine. The thing with my family is they are all a bit off the rails, my dad for instance, he is a heroin addict. And so that he can afford to get more he sends my 15-year-old sister out to work the streets by night and steal by day. She is alright herself but doesn't have much choice about doing the things for him as he would severely beat her like he used to.

My mum unfortunately died when I was only about 2 years old and that is when my dad started having problems. At first when I was about six it wasn't that bad, just things like alcohol and cigarettes, but this all changed when he met the worst person in the world (my stepmum). She used to take cocaine and my dad fell for her and also thought he could help her. But unfortunately things went the other way and she got him into drugs.

So as you can see I am the only sane one left in my household. I've been thinking about running away for a long time but I'm scared about what will happen to me if my dad finds out and manages to get me.

My plan for the future is to hopefully get as far away from here as possible and maybe move to America or Canada and be a social worker so I can help people who are stuck in the situation I am currently in. But this means I will have to work extremely hard to do well in school and save up money once I have left which isn't easy to do when you come home to what I do every night.

But I'm determined to make this happen.

Matthew Phillips (14)
St John Fisher RC School, Peterborough

A Day In The Life Of A Mouse

The biggest obstacle in the way in the day of a mouse is the large, tall, fat, fluffy cat that sleeps by the fire on the sheepskin rug. The other threat is his owner who has left a piece of chocolate on purpose, thinking I might go and get it, being furry, small and hungry.

I must hurry as the cat might wake. Just before my mother went to snatch something she would say, 'I must hurry, must be quick. Just a sniff, just a lick, just a bite, thought I might, zoom, just before the light comes on, wouldn't even know it's gone'.

Filled my belly nice and full, over to my cosy hole in the skirting, up between the floorboards I go. In my snugly nest I go to lay my head and rest. Curled up in a ball, do not wake before nightfall.

I have to use my wits at night to quietly get about, pass that ginger beastly cat who sometimes waits behind the cat flap. He thinks he has outwitted me but I'm too quick and small. I have lots of exits in and up the wall.

I quietly sleep through the day, not a squeak, not a peep from this old mouse. I gently breathe in and out just waiting for the night for . . .

'Just a bite, thought I might, zoom, just before the light comes on, wouldn't even know it's gone'.

Josephine Caulkett (13)
St John Fisher RC School, Peterborough

A Day In The Life Of A Baby

I was so happy in my mother's womb, so warm. I know that I was getting fed. I was so happy, *until* . . .

One day, just as I was settling in for the night I felt this rumble. I was so scared. Knowing I was going to leave my mother's womb, frightened me. I realised I was being forced out of my home to join these species in white shirts.

I tried and tried to push myself back into the place I called home. That lady was having none of it. She was screaming, almost as if she wanted to get rid of me.

The eagle has landed. These species were staring at me with this weird expression on their faces. I gave one look at them and screamed. I screamed once, and I screamed twice. I begged these things to let me go home, but instead they placed me in a flat container - which I wasn't used to. The species called it a cradle. These species placed a bunch of fluffy, soft, great huge items in the cradle with me. They were surrounding me.

I tell you now, the planet I have landed on is horrid. To make it worse I'll tell you about the drips. I call these two things drips because drips leak and these things leaked a *lot!* This thing was placed on my head. It forced my mouth to attack the drips, so I attacked. The drips had this white-coloured liquid, which they sprayed into my mouth. Now I must confess I kind of liked the taste. After our war where I chewed and the drips sprayed we became friends. I suck on the drips quite often, now I think about it.

For now I just deal with this planet who took my home. I'm prepared now, for when the men in white come my way and attack.

Monel Anderson (13)
St John Fisher RC School, Peterborough

A Day In The Life Of A . . .

Being a tree wasn't that bad. Well, that's what I thought for a few hours of the day.

It was nice seeing different kinds of animals passing by in the middle of the forest. Some animals just came under me to rest. They did not disturb me, but later on came a bird which pricked me continuously. I think that bird was called a woodpecker. It was so annoying that I could almost break into a half. I'd have shouted at him if I'd had a voice.

Right after, as he left after a few minutes, well I think it was minutes but they seemed like hours, I had a short sleep of about a few seconds when I heard this terrible noise. I didn't know what it was but I was sure it was from somewhere near me.

This tree friend of mine that I had met earlier this morning said, 'Oh it's that funny-looking man with that weird-looking thing in his hand again which is killing all the trees.'

I thought for a second, and then asked, 'Is he going to kill us as well?'

The tree friend replied, 'I don't know, it might.' He sounded a bit frightened and so was I.

Later on I realised the terrible noise was coming nearer. I just wished it wasn't heading for me when I saw the man - and the weird thing, the tree friend was right, he looked funny!

He came nearer to me and then nearer and opened the weird thing. Ouch, this hurts, nooooo.

Sakina Giaffer (15)
St John Fisher RC School, Peterborough

Madrid Mayhem

I was really excited; I couldn't wait to get to Madrid. I was going by train to meet my boyfriend Luke. Mum wasn't happy about me going, she'd said, 'You're only sixteen, you shouldn't be meeting boyfriends, you're not going!'

How could I have been so stupid? Why didn't I listen? He could have visited me, I should have stayed! I wouldn't be in this mess for a start . . .

Stacey, my best friend and I were just sitting down from going to the toilet, when we suddenly heard screams. Shouts, crying, footsteps! Then, without warning, a massive loud bang. I could see flames spreading fast. We didn't know what to do or what was happening.

Stacey was crying now, we were hiding under the table, in the back carriage. People keep running through. We were all packed in together, in one little carriage, squashed and scared. I couldn't see the flames anymore, but I didn't think they'd gone out, I hoped they had.

Stacey was shaking again, I felt scared and frightened. No! No! It's coming! It hasn't stopped! Stacey are you still here? The smoke, I don't want to die, help, someone, please . . .

That was all that was found written on the side of the carriage, unfortunately Stacey and her best friend Emily both died.

Lucia Seery (13)
St John Fisher RC School, Peterborough

A Day In The Life Of Gilbert

Bang! The changing room door slams open! Gilbert wakes up in a fright hearing the players come in. Gilbert starts to get excited, Predator and Rhino haven't heard them. Gilbert works his way to the top of the bag trying to make as little noise as possible, he can now see the players. They are all smartly dressed in shirts and ties, talking to one another and starting to get changed into their kits.

A man walks in, chucks a big bag on the floor and says, 'Shirts on lads.'

The lads then begin to search through the big bag looking for their shirts.

'Kick-off in half an hour,' blares one of the players.

Gilbert is getting really excited, he starts to sing to himself, 'I'm at the top, they're gonna pick me, oh yeah!'

The players walk out of the changing room without him, Gilbert starts to cry. *Why haven't they picked me?* he thinks to himself. Then suddenly *bang!* the changing room door opens and there stands the skipper - Rodney. Gilbert can see him searching around the changing room for a ball, he thinks, *this is my chance,* and rolls out of the bag towards him. Rodney picks him up and runs out of the changing room and onto the field.

'Yes, yes!' Gilbert shouts. 'I'm on the field, my first match ever.'

Gilbert is given to the ref, he places him under his foot and calls the two skippers.

'Maroon you're heads, grey you're tails,' shouts the ref. He tosses the coin high into the air which lands next to Gilbert. 'It's heads,' yells the ref.

Maroon No 10 picks up Gilbert who tenses up, Gilbert is then booted into the air. Grey No 6, Charlie, catches Gilbert securely in his arms, and runs forward towards the maroons. Charlie is tackled hard and Gilbert flies up into the air landing into the open arms of No 4, Matt Edwards, who then passes him out to the wing. Gilbert now lands in Ali's hands. Gilbert feels very dizzy and can't see where Ali's going. The next thing Gilbert knows, he is rolling around in a sloppy pool of mud, then the pack come down on top of him like a ton of bricks. Poor Gilbert is knocked unconscious, when he finally wakes up in a daze he hears the half-time whistle being sounded.

The grey team are in a huddle in the middle of the pitch, Gilbert is inside the huddle being kicked around by a few of the players who are winning by 12 points. The score is maroon 7, grey 19.

'I've scored 4 tries,' Gilbert grumbles excitedly to himself.

The match was over, both teams went on to score another try each. Gilbert felt dizzy but was also very proud of himself, he was feeling sleepy and wanted to rejoin Predator and Rhino in the ball bag, in the changing room which he did a few minutes later, when the team returned to get changed. Gilbert was placed in the bag to be congratulated by Predator and Rhino. Gilbert the rugby ball fell asleep straight away.

Daniel Cooper (14)
St John Fisher RC School, Peterborough

A Day In The Life Of A Soldier In WWI

The sound of shellfire woke me up this morning. It always does. I tried to go back to sleep, but the sergeant came round and barked at us to get up. I sleep in what can only be described as a pit. It's damp, cold and muddy, the same as the rest of the trench really. There're only planks of wood on the ground to stop us sinking into the sodden mud. They never work anyway. There is often water up to our knees, so it is very hard to move around.

As I got my breakfast of cold bacon and a piece of stale bread this morning, there was a gas attack. This meant I had to drop everything (literally, I had no breakfast this morning, thanks to the Germans) and squeeze a tight gas mask over my head. This so-called 'gas mask' is just like a bag with 2 eye holes and a filter to breathe through. Not that you can breathe in them. It's almost suffocating being inside them.

By the time the gas warning was over, it was my turn to do sentry duty. Sentry duty is basically standing on a ledge occasionally poking my head over the top of the trench to see if any Germans are offering themselves up to die. As you can tell, this doesn't happen very often.

Sentry duty takes up most of the day, so it's supper time when I've finished. Stale corned beef is on the menu today.

Leo Healy (14)
St John Fisher RC School, Peterborough

A Short Story

My story is about my niece, Niamh. She was born yesterday morning at quarter to four and weighed five pound 13 ounces. Luckily for my sister there were no complications. I think she is really cute, but then again, when she's your own family, they always are the prettiest or the strongest or the best behaved. It still feels strange how I've got a new niece, as my sister already had a son.

My nephew is two years and ten months. He was born 28th of May 2000 at nine o'clock and there were minor complications, but both baby and Mummy were fine in the end. My nephew is called Jack, he can talk perfectly and has no disabilities. I think he's still a bit confused. He keeps on saying 'Mummy, Niamh go home soon?' and we're all like 'No Jack, Niamh lives here now!' I think he just finds it weird sharing his mum.

As for me, I'm loving it! All my friends are saying, 'I wish I had a niece or nephew.' I just smile but inside I'm like 'Yeah! I've got a nephew *and* a niece!' It's all good. I go round most nights after school to help out with Jack, and now I will with Niamh. I will give my sister and her husband all the help and support they need. Even though they are doing fine, they probably think I'm just interfering! But I love them all!

Carla Corrado (13)
St John Fisher RC School, Peterborough

Warble Williams And The Pink Pelican

Warble Williams lived alone in a small cottage in a village just outside Dorset. He owned a little farm with his friend Jelly Johnson and together they owned 4 hens, 2 cows and a bull, 7 sheep and 1 horse. Jelly watched over the farm and Warble Williams would feed the animals, but they would always go to look at their crops together and every year they would both climb into the tractor and harvest, then they would sell the crops and then plant more for the following year. Each year they would buy 1 more hen, a cow and a sheep just so they would have healthy livestock in years to come.

Warble moved into the farm with Jelly and just as the year before he watched the lambs, calves and chicks grow and then he went to market, and that is where he saw the pink pelican. Warble Williams had never been adventurous but he brought the pelican along with all the usual animals that he usually brought with Jelly.

Warble built a pond for the pelican; he placed reeds in the pond and tried to encourage other animals to venture into the farm. After a few weeks, the pond was overrun with wildlife and people started to come and look at what Warble Williams had created. Eventually he opened a zoo for wildlife, and people came for miles just to see the wildlife and the one pink pelican.

Charlotte Walton (14)
St John Fisher RC School, Peterborough

Twinkle Big Bright Star

Me and my friends decided to go out for a long walk as it was a breezy sunny day. The sun was blazing and the air felt fresh, the wind was gently blowing in my face whilst my hair was blowing in front of my face.

We were walking for ages across a big field of bright green grass with the odd daisy scattered. I suddenly noticed in the bright blue sky with a few fluffy clouds which looked like cotton wool, a bright star. It was coming towards us. My friends started to get scared and they ran off but I don't know why, but I wasn't scared so I just stood there.

All of a sudden, it fell to the ground and a dark shadow came out of it and said to me, 'Everything's going to be alright!' Then in a flash everything was gone. All I could think of was a relative of mine that had recently died. I was really sad when she died because we were really close. When they had disappeared I stood there with a smile on my face.

I knew it was a sign from my auntie so I felt alright. I didn't tell anyone what happened, but every night when I look out of my bedroom window, I see a big bright star twinkling and I know who it is .
. .

Gemma Danile (14)
St John Fisher RC School, Peterborough

Fame Fantasy

There I was, standing in a bright studio, watching people rushing around behind a dozen cameras like bees in a hive, everything suddenly went still and quiet.

'So,' said a tall man with spiky blonde hair, 'can you give us any sneaky information about your upcoming film?'

Words rolled off my tongue as though I'd been practising them for the last two weeks. I had no idea what I was saying, or what was going on around me.

After my speech, the lights dimmed and everyone seemed to start rushing around again. I felt someone pat my shoulder as a little woman in shiny black high heels walked up to me.

Fantastic! Absolutely brilliant, there are refreshments in the room just to your right over there!' she said, her bouncy flame-red hair bobbing up and down as she spoke. I could see the tall man laughing silently to himself.

I felt a sharp pain in my left arm. Then I awoke. I could barely see the outline of the doctors and nurses around me as they injected me with a thick fluid. The white room and bright lights hurt my eyes. Tubes had appeared from nowhere; all the nurses had a look of deep concentration, but at the same time, wore an expression of extreme relief. Then I saw her: my mother. She sat there, tears streaming down her rosy cheeks.

'W . . . welcome back,' she stuttered.

Erin Tunney (14)
St John Fisher RC School, Peterborough

A Day In The Life Of A Teddy Bear

Hello, my name is Bert and I'm a large, fluffy, brown teddy bear. I belong to a young, six-year-old girl called Emily.

I first met Emily when I was young. I was sitting on the shelf in 'Betty's Bears' when Mr Jones walked up to me and said, 'You're a smart-looking bear. Emily would love you.' He bought me and I was wrapped in pink paper and tied up with a pink ribbon. I was Emily's birthday present.

Every evening at 7 o'clock, Emily comes to bed and cuddles up to me. When she falls asleep I wriggle out of her arms and settle at the end of the bed to go to sleep myself, because it's a tiring job being a teddy!

Danielle Roberts (13)
St John Fisher RC School, Peterborough

Being A Bird

Just imagine life as a bird, how do you think you would feel? I'd probably feel different because in this life there is not much freedom around me. In the life of a bird you have lots of freedom and you get to fly to wherever you want.

However don't forget the bird's hunters, they will hunt you till they get what they want and that is all the birds. Even though you have freedom you also have to watch your back and be careful just in case the hunter sees you.

Talking about flying everywhere just think how hard that can be. Imagine you are driving an aeroplane, think of the calculations going on in your head then. You have to calculate the wind speeds, the pressure, the height etc. Being a pilot is hard enough, but this is a bird. Birds are small animals that fly every day against the windy, rainy weather. If you compare birds and aeroplane together, they are quite similar except birds do much more than aeroplanes.

Being a bird could be pleasant in the summer. Summer freshness up in the sky, that's probably all you can wish for. I guess whatever you are there will be bad points and good points in your life. Nobody's life can be perfect you just have to deal with it.

Yodapa Pullsri (13)
St John Fisher RC School, Peterborough

India Triumph Over Pakistan

India wrapped up the one-day series against Pakistan with a gruelling 40 run win in the final match in Lahore.

Laxman hit a masterful 107 off 104 balls to lead India to 293-7 after they were invited to bat by Pakistan.

The news skipper Sourav Ganguly could miss the first Test after injuring his back soured India's win. Ganguly was said to be in 'intense pain' by team management after he ell attempting a stop at mid-off to counterpart Inzamam-ul-Haq, who scored 38 in the unsuccessful run-chase. Ganguly's pain, however, soothed by the efforts of his team, who came from 2-1 down to become the first Indian team to win a one-day series in Pakistan. India were 171-3 and well on the path to a formidable total when Ganguly fell to Shoaib Akhtar in the 33rd over.

Pakistan looked edgy at the start of their chase as they confronted an asking rate of almost six runs per over.

Malik (65) and Moin Khan (72) joined forces against India's threadbare attack to give Pakistan hope where they was none, putting on 99 in 97 balls for the seventh wicket - a one-day record for India against Pakistan to within 99 runs of victory in the 41st over, an equation which Moin and Sami (233 off 26) eroded to 48 off the last four overs.

The one day decider provided a tantalising precursor to the three-match Test series which gets under way in Multan on Sunday.

Aneesa Asghar (13)
St John Fisher RC School, Peterborough

How We Came To Have Curtains

Now everyone, well almost everyone, has curtains or blinds in their house. Well have you ever thought who thought up the curtain or how they came to be? Well let me tell you . . .

Once there was a man named Tom in the town of Swansea. Tom liked to play a game when he was small and the game was called 'Peeping'. What you had to do was follow someone around and spy on them through the window.

Also in the town lived an old widow called Curtain who one day caught Tom and his friends peeping through her window. She was so angered by this, that she decided to put up a net over her window so he couldn't peep but the net wasn't any good so the widow went to the tailor and asked if he had any material. The tailor only had some thick material so the lady took it. She then went to the carpenter and asked if he had any long pieces of wood. She then cut holes through the fabric and threaded it through the wood.

When Peeping Tom came back, he couldn't see through the curtains, this idea spread throughout Swansea and Tom and his friends had to think of another past time.

Zeinab Alliji (13)
St John Fisher RC School, Peterborough

A Day In The Life Of A Piece Of Bread

She's pulling me out of the brown Hovis bag that I have gotten so used to and she's spreading butter all over me, it feels so slimy.

I'm Penny the piece of bread and I'm going to be part of a sandwich. 'Urgh! I have a piece of ham on me now. My friend Herbert is put on top of the ham and . . . oh no! We're getting cut in half! Ow! Well I suppose I'm exaggerating a bit, it actually didn't hurt as much as I'd expected, now I'm getting wrapped up in tin foil and put in Lucy's lunchbox next to a packet of crisps, they smell like salt and vinegar.

On her journey to school, Lucy keeps swinging her bag from side to side which is making me feel quite sick.

At break time Lucy takes her lunchbox out of her bag and I tense up and feel very scared, her hand is getting closer and closer . . . and closer . . . and then she chooses an apple, it's alright I'm saved.

She puts her lunchbox back in her bag and goes back to lessons. I get so bored that I start to wish she had just eaten me so I decide to talk to Herbert, then suddenly we start moving again. Lucy sits down, takes her lunchbox out of her bag and unwraps the tin foil, she brings the sandwich to her mouth and chomp! *Nooooo!* She eats me, that's the end of my life, it's all over. I'm writing this from inside her stomach.

Virginia Tilson (14)
St John Fisher RC School, Peterborough

A Day In The Life Of Chaz

It all started when that silly fat shopkeeper opened the box of chewing gum and started stacking us on the shelf.

Luckily for us we were underneath a couple of packets. There was 8 of us in this one, Bob, Janis, Linda, Mark, Naomi, Alan, Peter and me, Chaz. I was good friends with all of them, I mean we had been processed together and everything.

All the kids were coming in the shop before they caught the bus to school, well unlucky for us about 12 of them wanted chewing gum. It was all going swimmingly until we were chosen by the little fat ginger kid with glasses as we could tell he obviously went through a lot of chewing gum because of his sparkling white teeth, I could see all this through the packet, they're quite see-through you know! But just like the rest of them, Fatty, we nicknamed him, chucked us right into his inside blazer pocket, which smelt nicely of Lynx at the moment.

It was about an hour and a half before he finally ripped us open and shoved Bob into his mouth, unlucky for Bob he was at the top. The packet was going down quite quickly, Janis, next Linda then Mark. We were nearly all taken.

Then it came to lunchtime, I was the last one left. I was trying to keep my spirits up but it wasn't easy after fatty had just done PE and quite clearly forgotten his deodorant. That was it, I was lifted very slowly and quietly, he was obviously in the middle of a lesson, Fatty slid me into his mouth which, can I say, was full of orange bits around his teeth, in his gums, everywhere, it was over in a flash, he tossed me around in his mouth about 18 times, then suddenly took me from his mouth and placed me on posh Penelope's skirt.

Fatty rubbed me in; I felt like saying, 'I'm worth more than that Penelope.' Penelope, crying, ran eagerly out of the classroom into the toilets. I had never been into the girls' toilets before and to be quite honest was enjoying it till posh Penelope got soapy water and started rubbing it into me, that hurt, it was really stinging my eyes, it also wasn't working so she ran up the corridor to the kitchen. I thought she was going to burn me off but worse than that, I was put into the freezer, it was so cold I was freezing.

The next I knew, I'm in the recycled clothes bin in Sainsbury's car park telling everybody about my ordeal.

Emma Cooper (14)
St John Fisher RC School, Peterborough

The Day In The Life Of A Rabbit

Flopsy, what a stupid name. They could have called me something like Buster. I mean Flopsy sounds like a girl's name, and *I am not a girl!* Oh no, here comes more screaming children. Anybody would think I was a clown the way they point and laugh at me. Just because I look different to all the others. They are all normal colours, not like me, I'm a blue rabbit. Blue, what a colour for a rabbit, I just wish I was normal.

'Look at that rabbit!' said one girl.

'Yeah who would want to buy him?' said another.

It's not just the people that are nasty to me it's the other rabbits as well. It's not what's on the outside or what colour I am that matters, it's who I am that really counts. I am not weird I'm unique. Like everyone else. But everything changed on this one day . . .

The pet shop was soon closing for the day and I had spent another day sitting in my hutch listening to people laughing at me but then someone came up to the run and started to stare, not making a noise but just standing there with her mother.

'Ahhh. Look at that rabbit Mum, can we get him please Mum please?'

'Yes of course we can. As long as you promise to take care of him.'

'Yes I will, I promise.'

I couldn't believe my floppy ears. They actually want me. I thought this day would never come, and it is the happiest day of my life. I couldn't stop hopping around. This was the start of a new beginning, a good life . . . or was it?

Emma Morrison (14)
St John Fisher RC School, Peterborough

A Day In The Life Of A Newspaper

This morning when I woke up I was on this huge sort of shelf thing. As I looked around there were loads of really tall people walking by. I didn't know what was going on, when suddenly I was lifted up by a large man wearing a suit and tie and he was carrying a huge sort of suitcase. I was really scared.

I was shut in the suitcase. It was so dark. I thought it was the end until after what seemed like ages I saw a blinding light. I was lifted out and flicked through a couple of times. I was dumped on the seat. I looked around and realised we were moving through the vast countryside!

After a while a bony-looking woman with her big bag came along. She dropped her huge heavy bag on top of me then lifted it back up and stared at me for a moment or two. She opened her bag and took out a pen. She started drawing circles on me. We started to slow down, the lady sighed and walked away.

I started to feel rummaged through enough and really fed up. When yet another man wearing a uniform and carrying a big black bag picked me up and threw me in the bag!

The next morning I woke up and I sniffed; I suddenly realised I was on top of a dump! I tried to escape but the more I moved the deeper in the rubbish I became. I realised that this was the end!

Laura Wiles (13)
St John Fisher RC School, Peterborough

A Day In The Life Of A Geographical Article Writer

I was exhausted from hunger and weariness. The thick custard of a desert was a drowning place of death as well as a geographical masterpiece. But I braved it, and called to Hannah with all of my strength about the desert. I enjoy this rare and exhilarating career destiny has brought me too.

We saw a little lizard and the desert dunes towered above the small cacti and thorny plants. That was all we saw today, and it is hard to encourage people to come to this merciless area of no scenery and hardship. We are running out of water and have lost our camp because of a sandstorm. This is just another day of struggle for survival.

Rebecca Digby (13)
Swavesey Village College, Swavesey

The Dragon Of The Sea

At the time when the first waters came upon the Earth there was a large, monstrous creature. The creature was larger than any creature created by the high spirits in the celestial realm. Neither was it created by the dark spectres inside the caverns, deep under the Earth. The greatest and most dangerous lord of all created it; Time brought it into being like everything else in power. But this creature was dark and had scales stronger than any stone, with a temper more violent and short than the thunder. This creature was the great Thyreticlator.

This Thyreticlator was created centuries before men. It had no true form, so no weakness was noticeable. It changed from spectre to dragon, to demon. Each form causing different types of chaos.

This creature was too mighty and the world was too young to cope with such a terrible creature. No god could destroy this creature, as Time did not wish the Thyreticlator to be eliminated. But Time decided to imprison the creature, until the world was old and the inhabitants gained power. Time gave the Thyreticlator a form, a large, black, grey and white dragon. The creature was placed under the sea, in a cave locked.

At the present the Thyreticlator causes whirlwinds, floods, waterspouts, and tornadoes. In the future it is prophesied that the Thyreticlator will rise and end the world and die ending the world. But Time may replay this world again and again.

James Barker (12)
Swavesey Village College, Swavesey

Through Her Eyes

A cold feeling of dread gripped Charli. She gasped for breath and felt her heart thumping weakly in her heaving chest. Her forehead felt cold and clammy, yet she could feel beads of sweat breaking out and dripping down her nose. Charli's vision blurred, yet it was only when the first droplet of water splashed down her cheeks that she realised she was crying. Grappling at the seat belt that held her to her chair with a grip like a vice, she clicked the metal tab out of its catch, and allowed it to zip up to its original place. Her eyes smarted, and slowly the gas smell around her turned to fire. Out of the corner of her eye, Charli saw flames spreading over the bonnet. She tried to force the door open, but it stubbornly held. Slowly, her grip loosened and the shoves grew weaker. The last thing she saw before her head hit the dashboard was the fire spreading closer and closer towards the windscreen.

Charli awoke suddenly. Squinting through the bright white glare, she pushed herself upright. Slowly the light seemed to dim, so Charli could see around the bed, a nurse was standing by her and she smiled at her. Charli could barely manage a grimace back. She slipped back down into the bed, a sudden thought washing over her, like a wave lapping gently over pebbles. She was safe, she was cared for, but most importantly, she was alive.

Katherine McLeod (13)
Swavesey Village College, Swavesey

A Day In The Life Of Shandy (Pony)

I wake with the large gleam of the sun, slowly opening my one eye, I gradually force myself up very ungracefully. I decide whether to find some grass or to go and kick my friend Jasper to persuade him to play.

Oh no, here she comes, should I make her chase me, which will make her angry, or should I let her catch me so I can eat some food? Ah, it's such a hard decision. Too late, I'm caught now I'll have to work!

Oh look, my food, let's go! Here she comes again but this time it's with my tack. Oh no!

Let's have a play with her when she tries to put my bridle on, I hate that silver thing that goes in my mouth. I have to do hard work now. I know, why don't I bite her bum when she gets on me? Yeah let's annoy her. 'Look everyone I'm the best let's go!'

'I'm all worn out now please take my tack off.'

I am slowly untacked. Good, now it's time for my dinner, here it comes, 'Mmm it's really tasty.' Oh no I have to go out to the field now. Bye-bye.

Aimee Jones (13)
The Beaconsfield School, Beaconsfield

Hamish The Hamster

9.47 Hamish the hamster wakes up.

9.49 Hamish nibbles on a few nuts.

9.51 Hamish stares dismally at the goings-on of the Patterson household, and wonders why nobody plays with him anymore.

9.58 Hamish comfort-eats a pile of sunflower seeds. Hamish is depressed. Hamsters shouldn't be depressed. They should be all bright-eyed and twitchy-nosed and excited. Hamish hasn't been any of these for a long time.

9.59 Hamish decides to get fit and healthy. He spends an amazing five minutes exercising on his shiny, blue wheel, before he is distracted by the cat, Mr Fuzball, his arch-enemy.

10.04 Mr Fuzball approaches Hamish's cage, smiling in an evil, cattish way.

10.06 Mr Fuzball growls and attempts to knock Hamish's cage over. Hamish hides and prays to the hamster god.

10.09 Mr Fuzball succeeds. Hamish's cage topples over and the cover pops off.

10.10 Hamish is cat food.

10.13 Mr Fuzball realises Hamish is still alive. Alive and chewing his way out.

10.15 Hamish is very much alive and Mr Fuzball is on his way to the emergency vet's with a large hole in his stomach.

10.24 Hamish decides it's a hard life being a hamster, as he finishes his pile of sunflower seeds, happily.

Lois Loxton (13)
The Beaconsfield School, Beaconsfield

A Day In The Life Of Badger The Horse

Today is Saturday and I am eating some grass in the field. There is someone coming into the field, and she's not alone . . . she's got a headcollar! I hope it's not for me . . . she's getting closer . . . oh no she's caught me . . . just as I was going to run away and make her chase me! Now I've got to go and do work!

I am being groomed now, that's not too bad, uh oh here comes the thing that every horse fears . . . the tack! Being ridden now but we are only walking at the moment.

'Badger forward to trot,' says Liz.

Oh sugar lumps, I hate trotting! Phew that's over, everyone else is trotting now.

Half an hour has gone and the lesson is over. Many lessons have now been and gone and I am getting untacked now, goody I can breathe again! (I can breathe but you know what I mean).

The rug is now on and here comes the dinner! Mmm that tastes scrummy.

10 minutes have gone and I have finished my dinner. Hannah is taking me up to the field now so I can go and play with my friends. I get some days off . . . until Tuesday comes! (mmm grass!)

Hannah Parsons (13)
The Beaconsfield School, Beaconsfield

The Very Smelly Cockroach

Ralf the cockroach was very much like any other cockroach. He liked to play outside, learn about the big wide world and most of all he enjoyed eating, just like everyone else. But that's the thing, Ralf was born with very peculiar tastebuds. All the other cockroaches liked sweet things, for example cake and ice cream, Ralf on the other hand enjoyed very, very smelly things especially smelly cheeses and fish. Ralf didn't care that he didn't eat the same things as the other cockroaches but he did care that he could never seem to make friends and this he just couldn't understand.

One winter's morning his mother sat him down and told him that he would never be able to make friends if he kept eating the way he was. Ralf gave his mother a perplexed look, and she said, very bluntly, 'You can't make friends because, well your breath, well it stinks!'

Ralf was mortified. 'What can I do?' he exclaimed.

Ralf tried a large variety of non-smelly foods but he couldn't find one to satisfy his tongue.

One stormy night Ralf was experiencing another nightmare about his breath when he was awoken by a tap on the shoulder. Ralf slowly opened his eyes to see a small shimmering fairy hovering before him. 'Am I still dreaming?' Ralf mumbled.

'No, I've come to sort out your smelly breath problem,' said a small voice.

'Who are you?' wondered Ralf.

'I'm your fairy godroach.'

'Of course, right I've been waiting to hear from you, I take it you got my letter pleading for your help?'

'Yes I did,' replied the fairy, 'and I have a solution to your worries.'

Ralf beamed with happiness.

'All you have to do is use this toothbrush and put a little toothpaste on it and clean your teeth and all around your mouth after every meal and your breath will smell as sweet as pie!'

'Fantastic!' shouted Ralf. 'Thank you so much, see you again soon!'

And the fairy flew off into the black night.

And from then on Ralf made friends as quick as a flash and never worried about his breath again.

Catherine Strawa (12)
The Beaconsfield School, Beaconsfield

How The Shark Got Its Fin

One day, a beautiful shark named Sakita was swimming the clear seas surrounding the island of Greece. She was the most beautiful shark you would ever see.

Not far away from Sakita was the greatest hunter of that time, he was called Obelix, he could get any animal he wanted if he put his mind to it.

That day Obelix wasn't looking for any animal in particular, when all of a sudden Sakita was swimming under Obelix's boat. He had never seen anything so beautiful and wanted Sakita for himself, he grabbed the nearest knife and launched it into Sakita's back, she struggled to swim but she sank to the bottom of the ocean with the knife still in her back. Slowly Sakita's health deteriorated and she died.

As from that day all sharks became vicious towards humans and as a warning they developed a fin on their backs and whenever a human was around they would keep their fin above the water as a warning sign to all humans.

Kelly Walker (12)
The Beaconsfield School, Beaconsfield

A Special Wish

It all happened one summer morning, I made a friend and got to see my dead mother, this is what happened . . .

I was sitting at home watching television, that was until I had to go to bed. I then had been asleep for about three hours and was having quite a good dream! However suddenly I heard a bang, which came from my closet, I sat bolt upright and swung my legs round. I was about to stand up when my closet opened, a girl aged about 20 years stumbled out and immediately said, 'Sshhh!'

'Who are y-you?' I said frightened.

'I'm Tilly the fairy, and I will grant you one wish under one condition,' replied Tilly.

'OK then,' I whispered.

'You must not tell *anyone* that you saw me,' answered Tilly, 'understood?'

'Yes, so does that mean I get a wish?' I said.

'Yes, you may!'

I started to think of all the great things I could have, chocolate, sweets, anything! 'OK, my wish is . . .' then I thought again and said, 'I would like to see my mum, she is dead and I'm missing her so much, can I?'

'Of course you can!' replied the fairy, with a tear in her eye . . .

Jessica Drummond (12)
The Beaconsfield School, Beaconsfield

A Child Called Thing

I just wanted to die, Dad was being even meaner than usual. I did not do my chores in time so I didn't get to sleep, that is three days running, I want Mum to come home and save me.

Dad caught me sleeping so I didn't go to school, which meant I was all alone with Dad.

Dad did not do anything, then when I thought I was safe, he grabbed my arm and pushed me into the kitchen.

Dad put my arm on the oven. It got burnt all over and was beetroot-red. Next he put TCP all over my burns, it stung, it really hurt.

Mum walked in and I thought I was saved, but she never did anything. She just sat at the table reading the bills and letters. Then Dad locked me out in the garden. I could hear them laughing.

I think Dad's crazy, or maybe I'm crazy, my life is crazy, I'm a thing, not a kid, maybe it's all my fault.

The children came home. I could hear them playing and having fun. No one looked at me, no one cared.

April Church (13)
The Beaconsfield School, Beaconsfield

Full Moon Mysteries

In the dark, dank town was a church. Not an ordinary church though, a meeting place on a full moon.

Midnight struck, the bells rang through the cold air. A cold wind blew over the town. The leaves rustled on the ground as a dark, dog-like figure scurried across the courtyard; it stopped and looked up as if expecting something or someone.

Two figures loomed across the moon. One with large bat-like wings, the other like black ink, dripped into water. They circled the spire and landed in front of the figure.

'You've come then,' said the winged shape in a stern voice.

'Of course she has. Why shouldn't she?' backchatted the flowing shape.

'Silence ghost!'

'For the last time, I'm not a ghost. I'm a spirit.'

The tall shapes bickered.

'Silence!' growled the crouched figure. 'Where are the others? They should be here by now.'

A high-pitched scream pierced the air. A flutter of wings, then a pink blur flew into the bush. The small pink shape crawled out of the bush.

'Oh sorry about that.'

'Call that a landing, fairy?' said the bat-like outline.

'Oh come Vampira, I'm not used to wings like you.'

'All we need now is Scarlett.'

As Vampira said that, a ring of fire appeared next to her. Twinkle the fairy hid behind the tail of the wolf. A swirl of black twisted, then dropped to reveal the last member of the group.

'I'm here, did anyone order a devil?'

Siobhan Hill (12)
The Beaconsfield School, Beaconsfield

How The Tortoise Got Its Name And Its Shell

Once upon a time, there was a peculiar animal. No one knew what he was called. His name was Tort. Tort had no friends and all the other animals played practical jokes on him. Tort was really depressed.

It was a cold day and Tort had nowhere to sleep so he went round to the snake's house and asked for somewhere to sleep. The snake said he didn't like Tort and he threw him out. Tort was small and had no furry coat like the other animals. He ended up sleeping under a tree.

Poor Tort went for a swim the next morning, he saw something gleaming at the bottom of the sea, he went to see what it was. Sitting there was a beautiful oyster shell, it was extraordinary and really big for a shell. Tort liked this shell and threw it up, it came tumbling down and squashed Tort. It stuck to Tort's back and he couldn't get it off. He went back to shore and thought that he looked good in the shell and he could sleep under it. He kept it on and he still does to this very day.

So that's how the tort-oise got its name and how it got its shell.

Matthew Tyson (13)
The Beaconsfield School, Beaconsfield

The Defeat Of The Vampires

3rd January 2023

A horrible screech of the alarm claxon echoed through the underground bunker.

'What's wrong Guinniz?' asked Jason.

'Activity in Transylvannia,' replied Guinniz.

The two spies ran for a small metal door and barged through.

'Did you fix the D-jet?' Jason asked with a somewhat doubtful tone.

'Yeah!' Guinniz replied.

The duo scrambled into the aircraft. It was a unique shape. Forward swept wings and at the rear, four colossal jets. It was jet-black in colour, polished and shiny. An immense array of weapons lay below the wings and inside the fuselage.

'You all strapped in?' asked Jason.

'As far as I know,' replied Guinniz sarcastically.

Jason toggled a few switches and the platform on which the aircraft stood, jerked and started ascending. As they reached the top, Jason gently urged the throttle lever forward. White flames burst from the jets and off they went.

Thirty minutes later:

'A mile to touchdown,' informed Gunniz.

'Okay!' said Jason.

'Right, land in that clearing.'

The D-jet landed vertically. The two crew climbed out, but suddenly an army of vampires leapt from the vegetation. Guinniz hastily drew his pistol and opened fire. Vampires all around, dropped, letting out screams. Jason clambered into the cockpit while Guinniz provided covering fire. The aircraft was soon in the air, dodging large rocks. The D-Jet took damage bravely. Jason released a cluster bomb and rammed forward the throttle and blasted through the sound barrier . . .

Thomas Poplett (12)
The Beaconsfield School, Beaconsfield

How Anteaters Got Their Long Noses

In the beginning there were the anteaters, for years they lived in perfect harmony. However, one fateful day a terrible natural disaster happened.

Years ago, before you were born, there were deserted wastelands for miles on end. There was nothing that lived there except for the anteaters.

The anteaters themselves were short, they had small legs with little waggly tails. Their main feature was their short stumped snouts. All in all the anteaters lived happily, quite content with life.

After a while the anteaters started to get worried, the ants were wise to their tricks. They used to roam around and the anteaters would eat them up. Now, however, they had started building ant hills. The anteaters' noses were not long enough to get down these hills. After a while the anteaters started dying and were becoming extinct.

The end was near for the anteaters, but something saved them. That something was a volcano. A mile away was a volcano, one hundred feet tall and it was very active.

The next day, smoke started to rise, molten lava ran out and the anteaters ran. They all avoided the lava but couldn't avoid the rocks. They came hurtling towards them and crashed onto the anteaters' noses. They all recovered but their noses never have. If it wasn't for the volcano they would be dead now, but with their long thin noses they can reach the ants in their hills.

So now if you're ever asked how anteaters got their long noses? You can tell them this great story.

Teresa White   (12)
The Beaconsfield School, Beaconsfield

SGI: From The Deep Supernatural And Ghostly Investigator

It was on the second night of the third month that the fourth disappearance occurred. The lake was still and dark. The only noise was that of Frank Hobble, slapping the oars of his boat against the surface of the water. He was out, gathering up the fishing nets he had cast that morning, observing the minuscule catch laid in the bottom of his boat.

Frank had once known of times when these waters thrived with fish - but no longer. He pulled out a flask of brandy and drank deeply from it. The warm liquid washing down his throat instantly reviving him from the chilly hand of coldness which held him. Frank did not see nor hear the long back gliding through the water towards him in his boat. It sent ripples far into the middle of the lake, sending a cold chill through Frank who was quite surprised by the sudden drop in temperature and took another swig. From behind him, the long sleek neck rose out of the water in an arch, followed by row upon row of razor-sharp teeth set in a head of pure muscle and bone.

It was casting a huge shadow over the miserly boat but Frank already knew his fate from the tales he'd heard and from the tight feeling in his throat. He still couldn't resist a look backwards to see the monster which nobody had ever lived to tell about, before Frank was another statistic of the lake . . .

Ryan Hall (13)
The Beaconsfield School, Beaconsfield

A Day With Twinkle The Cat

Twinkle the cat is ten years old and lives with his family, the Evans. Twinkle is well looked after, a little bit chubby, doesn't like mice and is very lazy.

It's eleven o'clock and Twinkle is still fast asleep dreaming of food. The Evans have just left the house, leaving him in peace.

Around about twelve noon, Twinkle starts to emerge from under his blanket. He slowly opens his eyes and plods along to where his food is waiting for him. Only thirty seconds and the bowl is empty with no trace of there ever having been food in there.

Off Twinkle goes to lie on the sofa for a nap. There he sleeps until the Evan's arrive then the house is filled with noise and laughter.

Charlotte de Morgan (12)
The Beaconsfield School, Beaconsfield

Little Red Wolf

One snowy day Little Wolf was wandering about in his cave looking for an adventure. His mother told him to lie down and get some sleep as they had to go out later to his grandmother's. He couldn't wait to leave, so when his mother fell asleep, he carefully wrapped around his neck, his trusty red scarf then slowly crept out of his cave, down the side of a hill leading into the dark woods. He kept to the shadows not wanting to disturb the animals and untouched snow which lay on the ground.

As he walked, he heard a sudden snap of a twig from somewhere behind him, he whipped round to see his follower, he looked . . . but no one was there! *Weird!* Little Wolf thought. So not thinking any more of it, he carried on, but a bit scared of what he might come across.

A few minutes later, he heard a loud roar from up ahead, he went to turn and run back to his mother where he would be safe but he decided to be brave and carried on.

There in the dark shadows, two glistening eyes stared back at him. He stopped dead in his tracks, the thing moved slowly out of the shadows, bit by bit. *What is it?* Little Wolf wondered . . . *argh! A bear!* Little Wolf was too scared to run, he simply stood there while the bear came towards him. The bear liked the look of Little Wolf's red scarf, he went to take it, so Little Wolf took it off and put it on the floor to protect it. The bear leapt on top of the scarf but couldn't get back up as he had hurt his leg. Little Wolf ran all the way to his grandmother's

When he got there, he told her all about his adventure. After he finished, she patted him on the head and told him how brave he was and surprised him with a new red scarf! With his new and trusty red scarf, Little Wolf settled down for a nap . . . as he drifted off he thought that it was hard being a wolf!

Danielle Piekielniak (12)
The Beaconsfield School, Beaconsfield

Captured

It's been a month since we started 'Mission Toy'. I'm already starting to lose the will to live. I'm cold and exhausted. We all are! We were about to abort the mission, it's been so long since we've sighted the Nazi soldiers.

'Quick! Take cover!' John whispered.

Nazi soldiers had perceived smoke coming from our campsite.

It was too late!

We were sitting in an army truck. Captured! We didn't notice that there was a whole military of soldiers. It was all down to Tim. That's why we're here. It was his obligation for the lookout on camp. Forty hours in pitch-black. The engine ceased. We got out, our eyes were bloodshot. We had arrived at the prison camp. We were stared at by soldiers that had already been imprisoned. The rusty hinges on the gate squeaked as hundreds swarmed.

'Where are you from?'

'What country do you come from?'

'What did you do?'

I just couldn't take it, they were viewing us like mass murderers. Why did I volunteer to suffer so much in so little time?

I think every night, *what if I could have changed the past?* But I've moved on - I had to.

David Jones (12)
The Beaconsfield School, Beaconsfield

The Alley

It was a cold dark night, Edward had just delivered some iced buns to his grandma, who lived on the opposite estate to him.

Edward was walking home, being swallowed into the charcoal-black night, when he came to The Alley. The Alley was Edward's worst nightmare but the only way to get home was to walk through it. Edward had heard the stories about the Alley. So he knew that it was said that anybody who walked down the Alley at night on their own, never saw the other side.

Edward's heart was thumping with fright, he had to get home and this was the only way. Edward took a deep breath and started to walk. This walk turned into a fast walk which turned into a jog, which turned into a run - which turned into a sprint!

He was halfway now, he turned back to see a dark figure emerging from the darkness. Edward screamed.

Edward's body was never found and he never saw the other side of the Alley.

Hannah West (13)
The Beaconsfield School, Beaconsfield

A Day In The Life Of A Cheetah

It's now twelve o'clock at night and I'm on the hunt. Selena, me and my one-year-old cubs haven't had proper food for days.

So many noises, crickets creaking, trees swiftly swaying in the wind . . . what's that noise? Something, something with hooves. I can sense. Where, where are you? I see! I'm crawling closer, the cold sending a chill down my back. Closer, closer, ready to pounce.

Silence, it's spotted me, the young yet big antelope has heard my footsteps on the grassy floor of the field. I'm going in for the kill, my mouth is watering and . . . go! I'm running, running fast, dodging round huge trees and spiky bushes as they get in my way. I can sense it's becoming tired as I chase it over fields and fields. Finally it slows down enough for my reach, I open my jaws and . . . !

Hannah Wilson (13)
The Beaconsfield School, Beaconsfield

My Short Story

Nick Parker crept up to the mound of snow in front of him. He looked over the mound and gasped, a massive castle stood before him. Its black battlements were home to hundreds of black caped men. On the castle's great gates, a thick layer of ice prevented anyone from entering. Its huge towers were guarded by specially trained Samurais, deadly in the martial arts. The almighty windows crackled against the wind.

Nick slid down the snow. His pure white clothes blending him into the pearly white background. He might not be able to get through the front entrance. Slowly he spoke into the transparent watch strapped to his wrist. 'Get all the men to the sewers.' Certainly the sewers provided a good undercover entrance.

'Check!' The voice muttered back to him.

Nick noticed the footsteps of his 200 back-up men. He was doubtful, even 200 SAS men might not be able to defeat the might of the Samurai warriors.

The men advanced on the castle, guns raised, ready to strike. Suddenly guns blared in the background.

'Duck!' Nick shouted into his watch. He ducked and whipped out his gun. The massive gates made a creaking sound. He turned slowly towards the gates. They were opening, ice dropped to the floor then shattered. Thousands upon thousands of fearsome warriors issued from the gates, bearing shining swords and jet-black pistols.

Nick crept around the battle, leaving his men behind.

'You think you can get away with this?' a voice said with hatred.

Then a gun fired . . .

Jack Bishop (13)
The Beaconsfield School, Beaconsfield

The Dragon Who Rose

A long time ago there was a dragon who attacked everyone, but there was one person who could stop it and who could save the world. His name was Cuban. The dragon was frozen by Cuban, he made sure that it didn't break free again.

But one night, the frozen dragon was cracking away and broke free and roared really loudly. Cuban heard the dragon so did everyone else.

Cuban got his sword and ran out of his castle, everyone was running as the dragon chased after them. Cuban said, 'This is between you and me!'

So the dragon just swung his arm and knocked Cuban over.

It was the next day when Cuban woke up, as he was knocked out overnight! It was not a pretty sight to see because everyone was dead because of the dragon.

Someone was coming down the hill on their horse and it was Lord Bagist, the most powerful man ever. He said, 'Come Cuban, come!'

They went to Lord Bagist's castle with his army and they went inside and talked.

'We will fight the dragon, although you cannot,' said Lord Bagist.

Just as Cuban was going to speak, the dragon smashed up the castle and carried on killing people

After a long time, the dragon was killed by another person and he was named king.

Dominic Long (12)
The Beaconsfield School, Beaconsfield

The Loved And The Lost

Keith stood as the cold, unforgiving waves swept past his feet. It was a day like this when his wife had passed away.

His wife, Lily, loved to swim. That day was a bad day to swim, the red flags were up and he told her not to go in but she swam until she was in too deep. She called for his help, but he couldn't help, she knew he couldn't.

One of Keith's mates saw him. 'Come inside!' he shouted. 'You need a cold, stiff drink to calm your nerves.'

It had been a year today that she had died.

'It's my fault,' Keith whimpered. 'I could have helped her.'

'It's not your fault,' replied his friend.

'Yes it is!' He stormed out to the place where the fateful accident had happened.

He started to walk away when he could hear her calling.

'Step into the water,' she called.

Keith hesitated, but slowly stepped into the water. It covered his legs.

'Deeper!' she called. 'Let the water swallow you.'

This time he didn't move.

Suddenly these two hands grabbed him and pulled him till his head hit the bottom of the ocean floor. Then he realised he could breathe!

So he lived happily with his wife and from that day on they were never seen again, and no one ever swam there again either.

Kelly Norris (13)
The Beaconsfield School, Beaconsfield

Untitled

Shocking news!

There have been a number of various sightings of 'The Object', but many people are still unsure of what they have seen. Through a vast amount of research we have come to the conclusion that the round light appearing in the sky is, in fact, the very unheard of 'UFO', meaning Unidentified Flying Object.

No one would have ever looked twice at this, until about 11pm on the night of Friday 13th, when a number of these objects started to appear in the skies over Beaconsfield Newtown. They were hovering over the people of the town for about 2 hours until they finally disappeared. Since then a number of crop circles have appeared around the town, but the one we are most interested in is the one that has appeared in the grounds of The Beaconsfield School, due to the fact that, alongside this sign, an abandoned spaceship has been found with footprints leading towards the building. This has now been happening in every school and town in the country, in the same pattern.

The only way people can escape is if they leave their homes and move near to somewhere that is beside a stretch of water. There are rumours that the aliens do not take kindly to this, as it will burn them if they are touched by it.

If people refuse to move, I'm afraid to say *the aliens will take over . . . !*

Kimberley Buckle (14)
The Beaconsfield School, Beaconsfield

Haunted House

It was midnight on the 31st October 2003 and there was a full moon in the misty sky and the wind blew making the bare trees sway spookily. The tall, wrecked, abandoned house shone in the moonlight. No noise could be heard but the creaking of the old house and the wind howling through the broken windows. Four innocent children, four *stupid*, innocent children, stood outside and stared at the house, not knowing what it had in store for them.

'So we going in or what?' asked Liam, no fear in him at all.

'Well,' hesitated George.

'Oh come on! You guys aren't gonna chicken out now are you?' Liam cried, walking towards the old, rusty gates.

'Course we're not! It just looks a bit dodgy, that's all,' replied Charlie, shaking a little.

'You'll be OK. Us two strong boys will look after you,' said Nathan putting his arm round Charlie.

She snorted and said sarcastically, 'Whatever you say Nathan!'

Nathan just frowned.

'Let's go in then!' cried Liam impatiently.

So the four of them walked through the gate that creaked loudly and crept up the gritty path to the front door which opened slowly.

'Spooky!' whispered George.

They all huddled together and shuffled into the house. It was dark, damp, smelly and there were pictures and statues everywhere, whose eyes seemed to follow you round.

'So, now we're here, let's do what we have to do,' whispered Nathan.

'We have to sit here and tell ghost stories. And we have to sit round a circle of candles!' explained Liam, who had lost his bravery.

So they all sat down in the middle of the room and lit a circle of candles in the middle of them all. Liam was the first to tell his story. It was about a girl who had entered this very house and slept there for a dare. Strange things happened that night and when her friends came to get her, she never came out and her ghost still haunts the house.

Suddenly there was a high-pitched scream, and a chill ran through the room. The candles blew out and the kids were left in complete darkness . . .

Amy Cutler (14)
The Beaconsfield School, Beaconsfield

The Path That Led Nowhere

I scraped my feet along the crisp autumn leaves, dawdling slowly home. I was thoroughly exhausted after another busy day at school. As I stumbled over a tree stump, I suddenly remembered Mrs Mead and her never-ending chess club - I was late. My mum had told me not to be late and I was already over an hour late. My uncle was coming back from Australia, I had always loved listening to his slightly eccentric stories of life 'down under'. We always treated it as a special event. It would take at least half an hour to get home this way. There was an alternative - the forbidding woods. Panicking, I tried to think of another option. I felt stupid; after all it was only a childhood myth. It mightn't be true and it was an emergency. I had made up my mind, as I turned towards the deep, dark, forbidding woods.

The wind howled furiously through the trees, sending shivers down my spine. I felt as if the trees were communicating to me through their whistles. Darkness was quickly approaching and there was an unmistakable smell of rotting earth. I felt trapped. Something was wrong, very wrong. It was all too quiet.

After an hour of wandering aimlessly through the trees, I began to despair. Was there any way out? Tears poured down my cheeks like a flowing river. Suddenly I felt the grasp of a large hand, cold and bony, on my shoulders. I turned round, my whole body gripped with fear . . .

Emily Harrington (13)
The Beaconsfield School, Beaconsfield

A Life-Changing Experience

People don't realise how every day is changing; from present to past. We are, however, more concerned about the future, what we're going to do, where we're going etc. This is exactly how we should be thinking in an ideal world. Judging what the next invention should be; flying cars, a new version of email, even robots!

One day a young teenage girl, Catrina was walking home from school, late, as she was obligated to stay back for her detention. On her journey home she witnessed a peculiar happening in the local park. She thought she was just dreaming and worked it out to be an alien but when it approached her closer it was actually some sort of a robot. This so-called 'robot' had been made and programmed to serve the public, in modern day English we'd call it a full time civil servant. Catrina carried on her journey home and acted as if it was just her imagination running through her mind relentlessly.

The following morning she went to do her weekly paper round and noticed the robot. She discreetly muttered to herself, 'Great, it's at it again!' She used personification to describe her mind.

The robot was serving the rights of justice by assisting an OAP cross the road. The robot saw Catrina and recognised her, so as predicted he strolled over to her, gently pulled her bag containing the newspapers and went around the neighbourhood delivering them. Catrina waited until he had finished before questioning him but he knew it was coming so before she spoke he gave her a sudden wink.

This bizarre experience in a young disobedient teenage girl's life, made her really think differently about the world and the way she lived her life. She joined an after-school club supporting nature and learned how to be more helpful to the environment.

It's amazing to see how something can really change your life.

Sinthuja Neminathan (14)
The Beaconsfield School, Beaconsfield

The Walk

It all started off with a teenage boy called Jack and his dad Dave.

The day started like any other, Jack got up, fed the dogs then did his chores. After this Jack and his dad went for their usual walk around the woods, just like they did every Sunday.

As they got nearer to the centre of the woods they jumped and fought through vast, thick foliage, when suddenly they came to a huge clearing, there were no trees and all of the bushes were crushed.

'How the hell did this happen?' said Jack. 'No vehicles could get in there, it would be impossible.'

While they were standing there thinking a fighter jet hovered above their heads then landed in front of them.

Suddenly two men got out, with guns pointing at Dave's head. They took him down and pushed his face into the mud. They said, 'Don't move or you will be killed.'

'Dad, what's all this about?' Jack shouted.

'Don't worry, just a bit of business, I'll be back.' And with that Dave and the two men left.

Jack ran straight home but when he got there his mum was drugged and his house was a wreck. Jack was devastated and worried. He had only one question in his mind. *What was happening?*

The next day Jack's mum was OK but his dad was still gone. Suprisingly, on the news he saw his dad. The headline read, 'Famous agent found dead with no possible leads'.

John-Webb Carter (14)
The Beaconsfield School, Beaconsfield

UFO In Wooburn Green

Story by Thomas Evans.

Yesterday in a small town called Wooburn Green, near High Wycombe, in Buckinghamshire a UFO was sighted in the sky above 'The Green'.

A woman called Wendy Ward said, 'It looked like a flying saucer. And it was like a CD, but bigger of course. I was really confused because I didn't know what it was until I heard people saying they're aliens and things like that. I was really scared after that', she said, 'it was really breathtaking'.

Another person I talked to was Robert Wells. He wasn't scared a bit. He thought it was just a hoax.

Was this a hoax or not? We asked a man called Malcolm Dennis and he said after some tests and interviews that there was not enough evidence to make a decision but it was probably unlikely.

Thomas Evans (13)
The Beaconsfield School, Beaconsfield

Noises

Sophie and her friends were sitting in their sleeping bags in the dark. They were in the living room, and were just talking about going on holiday together after they had done their GCSEs, when they saw the curtains starting to flap slightly and a low whistling coming from the door. Rachel, Sophie's friend, got up and walked nervously to the window and closed it, but that made the curtains flap even more. All of the girls huddled nearer to each other and fixed their eyes on the moving curtain. It flapped so violently that you could see the moonlit garden outside. The bare trees outside moved slowly in the wind.

The wind suddenly stopped. All the girls slowly lay down to go to sleep as they thought it was just the weather. Just as their heads touched the pillows the light flickered on and off, they all jumped. When the lights turned off the whistling became louder and when the lights were on it became very high-pitched and squeaky. The girls did not know how the door was making the noise as the door was firmly shut.

At this point they were so scared that they had to turn the light back on, but as they did so the flapping of the curtain started again. The light flickered and turned off and they were left in complete darkness. Suddenly there was a loud, high-pitched scream that came from one of the girls, then complete silence.

Jenny Prismall (14)
The Beaconsfield School, Beaconsfield

Crime In London Rises by 20%

The government last night looked at the crime rate in London. Tony Blair gave his comment on this terrible fiasco. 'It is absolutely disgusting!' exclaimed the furious Prime Minister. 'I don't know how this happened, only a few months ago the crime rate had gone down by 20%, now it has risen!' Adding to his comment, he insisted, 'We are all going to have to work together to once again, reduce crime'.

The Prime Minister was stunned to find that in recent questionnaires headed 'What do you think about London?' only 10% of the public would like to do something about the crime rate rising.

Tony Blair has resolved to increase VAT so that he can pay for more CCTV and employ more police officers. When the public heard about the tax rise they were horrified. They resented the idea of adding more tax to groceries, cigarettes and petrol.

The public are beginning to ask questions such as, 'If VAT is added throughout the country to finance extra police and more CCTV, are the police going to be employed everywhere or just in London?'

Tony Blair has admitted that he doesn't have the answers although has agreed to do everything in his power to be fair to the whole country.

The Prime Minister is challenged by the dilemma he finds himself in.

Reported by Abby O'Neill.

Abby O'Neill
The Beaconsfield School, Beaconsfield

My Friend Billy

My mum came home with a present for me today, I remember her getting out of the car, she slowly walked towards the door carrying a red-boxed parcel. She placed her key into the lock. I ran down the stairs to greet her.

She asked me to sit down so I slowly walked into the kitchen and sat down. She placed the parcel on my lap and then she stood back. I slowly lifted the lid and moved the tissue paper and there was the sweetest puppy ever. It jumped into my arms.

For the next few weeks I was full of happiness, love and joy.

The following Tuesday I was playing with Billy the dog, in the back garden. My mum walked into the garden to take the rubbish. She lifted the bags and waddled to the gate. The van came to collect them, but Billy ran out of the gate towards it. As I got up I heard my mum scream and silence fell . . .

Andrew McKenzie (14)
The Beaconsfield School, Beaconsfield

The Hollow Cave

A damp, pungent smell hung in the air around the mouth of the cave. Not knowing why I was here or how I knew the way, I wanted to leave but my legs wouldn't move. My heart thumped against my chest. As I took my first step into the cave, my head began to spin. The floor underneath was wet and slimy. I had to crawl on my hands and knees, because the stalactites were so low.

In the distance there was the faint sound of dripping water. It was so dark. My head collided with a corner. Slowly, I turned the corner as the stinging faded, and saw a bright light. I was so curious, where was the light coming from? As the light came closer, my curiosity turned sharply into dread. The dripping became louder and more intense. I managed to turn around but something was dragging me down towards the light. Even though I screamed as loud as I could, no one could hear me.

When I opened my eyes, the light was gone and the dripping was faint. My body was paralysed, there was blood on my face. All I could do was shut my eyes until the pain and fright went away. I shut my eyes till I couldn't feel anymore.

Alexandra Shrimpton (13)
The Beaconsfield School, Beaconsfield

The Mysterious Murders

Thames Valley police in Buckinghamshire have conducted a frantic search for a serial killer. This mystery murderer has, so far, killed eight married men in the space of five days. All the murders have taken place whilst the victims were either going to, or returning from work and bodies were all dumped in nearby rivers; which later washed up on the banks. The police have not yet been told by the coroners how the victims were killed but, we now know the maniac killer is not too fussed about leaving fingerprints. Unfortunately though the prints found are not on record.

All these murders are thought to be linked as they have happened within a week, in the same area. Also all the victims have been married for at least four years, and were between the ages of 25 and 45 years old. These chilling murders are very serious, so serious Scotland Yard have become involved.

Police suspect that the crazed killer is a woman, aged between 30 and 40 years old who is married or possibly divorced. They have reason to believe this because all eight wives (now widows) of the deceased had suspicions that their husbands had been cheating on them for at least a couple of months but never questioned them about it. Thames Valley police think the murderer's husband or ex-husband may have committed adultery whilst married to her, so therefore she may be getting her revenge on all cheating, married men she can find. So far they have only questioned two people in conection with these murders but they were later released free of any charge.

Here is what DCI Smith from Thames Valley police, in High Wycombe, who is in charge of the investigation, has to say. 'These murders are extremely serious and we desperately need secure evidence to catch this brutal killer. We would like to hear from anyone who may have seen anything suspicious around the Buckinghamshire area within the last week, or any information at all in connection with this murder case. Thank you. If you would like to make a statement or give any relevant information then please go to your local police station or call 0800 514 666'.

There will be more news on this in tomorrow's paper on pages 1 & 2.

Written by reporter Emma Dixon.

Emma Dixon (14)
The Beaconsfield School, Beaconsfield

A Day In The Life Of An Alligator

I was swimming in the water looking for some food. I saw a monkey coming up to the water. I snuck up underwater and attacked it. I killed it by gobbling it up.

I waited, then a boat came with two scuba-divers. They went very deep under the water. It was dark. I slowly swam up to them. But then they started swimming away as quickly as they could. I got one of their legs. He started to fall back down to the bottom of the water. His friend started to swim down to try to save him. When they both were at the bottom where you can't see more than 300cm the one I did not attack got stuck. I gobbled him up completely then the other people on the boat tried to shoot me with tranquilliser darts. I started to swim after them again. I chased them up to the boat and they got in, but I broke their propeller. They tried to use the boat to get away but their propeller was stuck. I got on the boat and went up to them slowly. One shot me with a tranquilliser dart. I tried to stay awake but I couldn't.

When I woke up I found out that I was in a zoo. I saw the people who had captured me, talking about me saying how hard I was to catch, I have a thumping head but I sort of like this place a bit more now.

Patrick Snaith (12)
The Beaconsfield School, Beaconsfield

The Minotaur

The Minotaur, sent down the unleashed to destroy cities with his axe that scrapes across the floor, as his horns knock down falling buildings, and his axe, small houses.

Many houses fell to this monster but none stood up to it until one little town that the Minotaur went to. As he approached he shook the Earth with his feet and knocked down two buildings with his axe, but that bought the city's patience to an end.

They all marched to the Minotaur attempting to destroy the mutant. Suddenly the Minotaur laughed and swang his axe. As this city stood up others came to save it with swords, shields, most with horses. The Minotaur was outnumbered by people - but not strength.

The people charged at him with swords hacking at his legs but not even a scratch appeared as he walked into the mist destroying more houses and killing more people.

The gods were standing at a halt as prayers to them were said. The gods had a meeting but meanwhile the Minotaur destroyed things laughing at pain and fear.

Suddenly the clouds moved as the gods poured down to destroy the Minotaur and succeeded. The Minotaur never walked the Earth again.

Josh Woodland (12)
The Beaconsfield School, Beaconsfield

A Day In The Life Of Polly

Today Polly is going to the stables like every Saturday. She wakes up at 8 o'clock and has her breakfast, gets dressed, does her teeth and hair, then gets her riding stuff out of the cupboard and puts it into the car. Then her mum drops her off and signs her in.

It's 9 o'clock and Polly is tying the hay nets on each of the tying posts and putting water next to them.

9.10am. Polly is getting the riding school ponies in from the field with help from the helpers. When all the ponies are in she feeds them breakfast. When they've finished breakfast Polly and the helpers groom them and tack them up.

10 o'clock. Polly is leading Fudgie in a lesson.

1.15pm. Polly is riding Fudgie, her favourite pony. Fudgie is a dun colour, she is about 13.2 and 6 years old. Polly likes cantering and jumping. Once she fell off and broke her arm and had pins put in it. Polly was seven then, now she's eight years old. In her lesson she is doing jumping. At first Fudgie refuses them. After a while Fudgie keeps on jumping over them. When she is ready they canter over them. The jumps are only small, one is 18 inches and the other one is 2 foot.

After the lesson she runs up the stirrups, loosens the girth, undoes the reins, then ties her up. Mum signs her out then they go home for lunch.

Libby Millar (12)
The Beaconsfield School, Beaconsfield

The Trip To Egypt

It was the summer holiday and I had gone on holiday to Egypt for four weeks. I went with my dad, mum and older sister who is 15 years old. We took the aeroplane from Heathrow to Luxor. It took two nights to get there. We stayed at a hotel called 5 Arms Likinshin. I unpacked my bags. I had to share a room with my sister.

After we had all unpacked we went to Cairo to see all of the pyramids, they were made from limestone. We had to take water with us, a bottle each, as it was very hot. It must have been 130 degrees. I had to wear a sun hat and put lots of suncream on. I had my flip-flops on and I could feel the sand. It was hot and my feet were killing me. We must have been walking for ages. We came to a spot under a tree, a palm tree.

Mum, Dad and my older sister rested whilst I played in the sand with a spade. *First I'll bug my sister by putting sand down her bikini top,* I thought, which I did and she started running after me. Later on she gave up and sat next to Mum.

I went to the pyramid that was near us and I started to dig. As I got halfway down, something stopped me. I dug on the other side and bent over to pick it up. The lid felt bumpy, with patterns all over it and there was also a crack in the lid. The box was heavy. I took it back to Mum and Dad, opened it up and there inside was a shell. Not just a shell, a golden shell. I told Mum and Dad and they said to keep it because it was worth a lot of money.

The very next day Mum and I went to see an archaeologist. I told him that I had found the box in the sand near a pyramid. What would it be worth and would he put it into the museum in Cairo so that people could see it and I could see it next year?

He told me it had been used by an Egyptian priest, he gave me $8,000,000 and put the box and the shell into the museum. I went home very happy.

At the end of the holiday when we went home I told all of my family and friends about the best holiday I had ever had.

Oh yes, I bought a new computer and TV for my bedroom and some videos as well. My family told me that I was the richest girl they knew!

Stephanie Richardson (14)
The Cedars Upper School, Leighton Buzzard

In The Wartime Hospital

Another day in the hospital has passed. I've never felt so helpless in all my life. The atmosphere is unbearable; the foul stench of death lingers in the air, mingled with sweat, and the blood which crusts men's bodies like black rust. You cannot imagine the nausea of standing by a doctor, trying not to vomit, as his bright knife slices flesh. And the horror of hearing the screams of grown men from the operating ward where amputations are performed. And the helpless sense of pity, at the sight of tense faces of mangled men waiting for the doctor, and awaiting the dreadful words, 'I'm sorry, soldier, but that arm will have to come off. Yes, yes. But see here now, it must come off.' And there's nothing to even ease their pain.

'Help me, Nurse . . . oh, please, give me something for the pain,' they croak at me, clawing at my skirt as I pass.

'I'm sorry,' I answer, 'but I haven't anything to give you.'

We're running out of beds. Many are lying on stretchers, some lying stiff and still, others writhing in agony. It frightens me; the look that death gives their sunken, sullen faces. Sometimes I just want to shake their corpses, stir some life back into their now motionless bodies. These are men that once thought and dreamt and hoped. Yet now, now they are nothing more than a name on a wooden cross. With each death, each last breath taken under my care, my heart seems to clench. Perhaps they are lucky to die, to escape from this surreal life where nothing seems good or true, and only suffering and fear seem to thrive. I am lost; I don't know what to do with myself when I'm not at the hospital. Everything I thought I once knew is fading, now only the dull thuds of coffins being flung into shallow graves seem real. The faces of the dead haunt me in my dreams, no matter where I turn, or what I do, their voices echo endlessly in my ears, and their hands reach out for me. At night I hear their pleas for water and feel their stark eyes once more upon me . . . they wait for me around every corner, they follow me wherever I go, their shadows just out of sight, their whispers just too low to hear properly . . .

My head aches with tiredness, my mind is numb, and so are my legs. It is all so grotesquely unreal, a nightmare. Pour water, serve food, clean the dead, bind wounds, mop floors and hold the dirty heads of the dying. I must sleep now, for tomorrow holds the same empty promise of the 'romance of nursing' and the 'valour of death'.

Georgina Taylor (14)
The Leys School, Cambridge

Being The Wife

(This piece of creative writing is based on a poem by Thomas Hardy called 'A Wife In London'. The poem tells of a wife, who receives a telegram to say her husband has died, yet the following day she receives a letter from him with regards to his hope for the future. This piece is her diary the day before she receives the telegram.)

I don't know what to think. My body is not functioning properly and I am constantly restless and fidgety. I just don't know what to think. I hope he's still alive, but war is so terrible and there has been such great loss, it seems impossible for him to have even a small chance of living.

Each day I scour the newspapers for the names of the dead, to see if his is on the list, rereading each sentence several times over, to check I don't miss anything. But there's nothing. He's probably being buried as I speak: in some muddy, brown monotony in France, or Belgium, or where? I don't know where he is. I haven't heard from him for nearly three weeks. At the beginning of the war he used to write at least once a week, if not more. That's it. He's dead then. He must be. This is Hell . . . a nightmare . . . I just can't cope.

Outside, through the fog I see driving rain. How on this whole stupid world is that supposed to help? I'm angry, but so afraid. How can anyone have let it get this far? How can this be benefiting our country and prospering our future? It can't be, can it? There is no way in which this agony, this disgusting, vile agony, which is affecting the entire planet, is going to benefit anyone. War: it doesn't even deserve a name. It shouldn't be allowed to exist.

This week has been the worst week of my life - it can't get any worse than this. This is Hell . . . a nightmare . . . I just can't cope any more.

Emma White (13)
The Leys School, Cambridge

A Day In The Life Of A Chair

Today I was woken up by the registration bell and the stampede. I wondered who would sit on me today in . . . registration. Since I have no eyes I can only smell so that is how I know who they are and today it was Zac, nooo! I can hear and every now and again there was a particularly rude noise, a laugh and a smell for fifteen minutes, yes fifteen whole minutes and finally the bell went and I was moved to a maths room . . .

Maths

I was carried and put down. Someone sat down who had a strange smell, I knew it was a girl, uh oh, they are strange, all of my scratches have come from girls who had been writing notes under the table and this girl was Toni. She had to write a note, didn't she, and sure enough, scratch, scratch, oh nice, they were actually going through the paper. Now I know who she fancies and who she thinks is fit! Then she decided to put some make-up on but missed, oh well pink's OK, well sort of and then the bell rang.

French

Yet again I have been moved to French and someone has sat on me called Simon, rather fidgety, loud and rude, I was constantly trying to keep my balance as he swung back and then he must have done something bad. I felt him get up and I was thrown across the floor and I landed in an awkward position, upside down, then I was picked up and put down. The rest of the lesson was quite pleasant then I had a break because no one sat on me because they were all out for break.

James Nicholas (12)
The Neale-Wade Community College, March

The Day Of The Black Sun

Today at 10.30am, driving on a summer's day in New York, our 42nd President William B Sheridan was shot three times in the chest.

The President died hours later from blood loss. The police closed off the roads for a 2km radius.

Later when the FBI searched an apartment 500m away from the President they found a Garrand MK9 with binocular scope sniper rifle with three bullets missing from the cartridge. The gun was also warm.

To all Americans this is truly the day of the black sun. The only known footage of the assassination was by a man who is now a millionaire from it.

The FBI think they know who it is and what foul terrorists caused this dark day, and would like any help they can. Their number is 55911-FBI.

William B Sheridan's brother Luke W Sheridan will carry on what he calls his brother's legacy. 'I will find the people who've done this, I will have a national mourning day and I will carry on with my brother's legacy'.

Jacob Bell (12)
The Neale-Wade Community College, March

A Day In The Life Of The Prime Minister

After receiving the wish that was sent to me so I can have a day in the life of anyone in the world, I thought long and hard and after great consideration I have decided to wish for a day in the life of the Prime Minister.

I would settle all the problems in Britain and make sure the number of crimes went down, I would visit unfortunate countries and make sure poverty was not an issue, I would start a fund-raiser so schools and shelters can be built in such places. I would also try my hardest to make sure everyone was treated equally no matter what race or religion.

After knowing that I have played my part in the world I would feel happier in myself and be proud. This day would also increase my knowledge of my luck to be as I am today.

Chantel McCullough (12)
The Neale-Wade Community College, March

A Day In The Life Of A Popular Person

I'm woken up in the morning by phone calls, people from school asking if they can sit near me at lunch. I never really know what to say - maybe, I'll see you there. What would you say?

I get ready for school, do my hair and get dressed into my so-called designer clothes. Then I walk to the bus stop.

The bus arrives at 8 o'clock I climb on and sit at the front, it's a two-seater. I say to myself, 'Here we go again.' Two boys from school fight over the seat next to me. I say, 'The seat's saved.' They walk away.

We get to the next stop, my friends walk on, I get up and walk to the back of the bus so me and my real friends can sit together.

We arrive at school at 8.30 where we get off the bus together and walk through the school gates.

Everyone rushes towards me.

'Hi Chloe!'

'Do you want to stay at my house this weekend Chloe?'

I walk straight through them holding on tightly to my friends. I walk to my locker.

One of my friends says, 'I wonder if you'll have as many notes as yesterday?'

I open my locker, they all fall over the floor. A boy rushes over to me.

'Shall I pick them up for you Chloe?'

I want to say no but my friends think it's fun being popular, but it isn't.

The boy picks up the notes and gives them to me, my friends say, 'You can go now.' He walks away and I shout out, 'Thank you!'

Toni Norton (12)
The Neale-Wade Community College, March

Creative Writing

One summer's morning in an army camp up in Scotland, there was a meeting between all of the commanders in the regiment. The meeting was about the Loch Ness Monster who was destroying people's homes and cars.

The Chief Officer of the army camp told all the commanders to get their men together and to go and kill the Loch Ness Monster. 'This is going to be a tough challenge for all of us because the monster is so powerful,' said the Chief Officer.

The next day all of the army camp set off to go and stop this powerful monster and they took everything with them, like guns, knives, tanks, jeeps and food etc.

They soon arrived at the site where the monster lived, after thirty minutes of travelling. When they got there they unpacked all their equipment and tents and set it all up.

All of the men stayed alert for a long two days to wait until the monster arrived back at his home. The men waited and waited, then after five days of waiting, the monster came home.

The soldiers jumped up with all their weapons and gear and started shooting. The monster turned round to face them and roared with anger. He then started coming towards them. Most of the men stayed focused and kept on shooting whilst some of the men were shaking with fear. The monster got really furious and started blowing sparks out of his mouth. The monster was surrounded by men who kept on firing missiles at him. Even the helicopters started coming in to help kill the Loch Ness Monster. The men kept on shooting and then suddenly the monster blew about five mouthfuls of fire onto fifty of the soldiers who died instantly.

Eventually the monster was dead, thanks to the twenty tanks which drove in and killed the monster who was destroying everything. He was finally killed after a week of fighting. All the soldiers left the lake the next day and went back to the army camp.

When they arrived at the camp there was another meeting.

The Chief Officer said, 'Well done men for completing your challenge, but sadly we lost some men in battle.'

Andrew Wright (12)
The Neale-Wade Community College, March

The Disappearing Act

You've read the title and you're probably thinking that it involves a magician - it doesn't! You see it's about something far more difficult and strange, very much so in my eyes. My name is Cara Dunlop and I'm fifteen and this is my story.

I live with my mum (Danielle) and my dad (Robert) and also my sister (Katie). I live in a small town called March, that's in Greater Cambridgeshire and every Tuesday I go to ATC, the Air Cadets, and that's where it all began.

It was an ordinary Tuesday . . .

'Cara, you're going to be late if you don't get a move on,' yelped Mum.

'I'm coming! Oh yeah, was that Jackie on the phone?' I yelped back.

'Yes darling,' she said, 'she can't come tonight,' Mum said.

But oh no, that meant I had to walk by myself. I hate going to places by myself.

I soon arrived at the Air Cadets and saw some of my other friends who went there. I went over and started to chat.

'Hey Zoey!' I said.

'Hi Cara, where's Jackie tonight?' Zoey replied.

'She couldn't come,' I sadly replied.

That night we didn't do a lot and every five minutes I was staring at the clock dreading the moment the clock struck nine.

Ding, ding, ding, ding, ding, ding! 9 o'clock! My journey home would now begin. But the worst thing was that as soon as I went round the second bend, someone was following me.

I walked faster and faster, sweating like a pig. Argh! Someone pounced on top of me. I didn't know who it was because they were wearing black. It was over in seconds and I got up and walked home.

I turned the key and hoped that Mum wouldn't give me any hassle and let me go to bed. As I stepped in I noticed everything was different. I closed my eyes and then opened them again but everything was the same. 'I'm in the wrong house!' I remember screaming.

I stepped upstairs and went into my room.

When did I put up pictures of cars and women in their underwear? 'I'm in the wrong house!' I remembered screaming.

I sat down to calm myself again but when I stood up the chair was covered with blood. I looked down, I was bleeding . . .

I've been stabbed, I thought.

Charlotte Roberts (13)
The Neale-Wade Community College, March

A Day In The Life Of Noah (Noah's Ark)

Dear Diary,

I have had a most concerning night. As you know, I am not a rich man and I am not a sinner but it seems that I am the only man left who is not a sinner. I tell you this for a reason. Last night as I was asleep, I had a dream - no it was more like a vision!

In the dream God told me that He would flood the world and destroy all the sinners. He told me that I need to make an ark and in it I should put all of my family and two of every animal, along with food and water. He told me that after the world was flooded, the waters would subside and my family and all of the animals in my ark would re-populate the world. I must start to make the ark as soon as possible, once the ark is completed then I will have seven days to collect a pair of each animal.

Two months later:

Dear Diary,

The flood has come, it has been raining for three days now. I only just got all of the animals on board in time. We had a small bit of trouble finding them all but we did it in the end.

Dear Diary,

I have lost track of the date and time but the water levels are finally beginning to lower. I can see the tips of the mountains poking out of the water and we can finally see the sun instead of those dreadful storm clouds. God bless us all!

Reece King (12)
The Neale-Wade Community College, March

The Accident

The process took ages. I felt really scared. Here I was in the hospital. This day should change my life. The fact is - I'm getting a new leg! I know it sounds scary but I have to have one. I've had loads of funny looks from people in the High Street, I just hate it. I really do! But this was all because of the bullies. Here's my story . . .

That day I had to walk home. My mum and dad were working late like they always did. Anyway, as I turned down Park Lane, out of the bushes came Rick, John and Sam. They pushed me over onto the damp, cold concrete.

'Get off!' I screamed.

'No! Why should we?' they retorted back.

'Because there's a policeman over there.' I pointed.

They looked, I took my chance and ran. I could hear them panting and shouting behind me. They were closing in. Just as a corner came up, I felt a foot by mine and I went sprawling into the road. Just then a car came and it all went black.

When I woke up the pain was immense, I screamed. Then I went out blank again.

So here I am, sitting in a hospital bed with a very badly broken leg. I hate it. Now some nurses are walking over to see me. My time has come! You're probably wondering what happened to those bullies - prison for them! Money paid! Apologies! That's the way some people are.

Bye-bye!

Patrick Awolesi (12)
The Neale-Wade Community College, March

A Day In The Life Of A Bully Victim

I wake up dreading school. I cry myself to sleep at night because I don't want the next day to come - but it always does.

I walk to school and everyone's okay with me but when I step foot into a classroom, the bullying starts. No one understands how upsetting it is when your friends turn their backs on you.

The worst part of the day is when I'm walking home, I walk home all alone. Every night I get beaten up by the people whom I thought were my friends. They only do it because they're scared of what the other bullies might say or do.

In class today we read a newspaper article on a girl aged thirteen who had committed suicide, and people in my class were like - *why did she do it?* And I said to myself, 'I can understand why people do it.' But I couldn't go that far, it would just be easier if I'd never been born!

What is wrong with me? No one likes me and I don't know why! My friends were my friends until we got to secondary school and now three years later, nothing's been done.

When I'm at home, I can't tell my parents anything because they say, 'You bring it on yourself.' Which makes it worse.

No one knows how upset they make me feel. I'm so depressed I'm scared of what I might do.

Terri Kilby (12)
The Neale-Wade Community College, March

Keep On Believing

'Night-night Josie,' said her mother, Claire.

'Night Mummy,' Josie replied.

Josie's mother pulled her door to and then went downstairs. Josie was excited, it was her birthday the very next morning so she couldn't get to sleep.

An hour passed but she was still wide awake. She could still hear the distant murmur of the TV downstairs.

She heard a noise, a gentle tap. Josie thought it was the wind but then it happened again. Josie sat up and peered around her room. She loved her room, it was magical, it was all pink with hand-painted fairies darting across the room. Sometimes Josie pretended she was a fairy and played fun games with her fairy teddies and dolls. Josie climbed out of bed then went to the window, she slowly opened the curtains conscious of what she might find. 'Oh wow!' Josie gasped. 'Fairies!'

There were roughly ten delicate fairies. 'Hello Josie, we know it's your birthday tomorrow and we have come to give you your present!' Tinkerbell, the main fairy, explained.

'Oh wow! A present? For me?' Josie asked excitedly.

'Yes, come!' they all chorused.

Josie closed her eyes, then opened them again. She was amazed as she was in Fairyland! She'd dreamt about this day.

Hours passed whilst Josie and her new friends played games and did each others hair. It then dawned on Josie that soon she would have to leave. She was feeling tired, her eyes felt droopy and soon enough she was fast asleep.

'Happy birthday Josie,' Josie's parents said.

'Thank you!' she replied.

'Come on, open your presents!'

It was all over the presents, the food.

At night, Josie saw a card, a tiny one, and it read, 'Dear Josie,

We all hope you had a good time with us. Keep on believing and we will meet again.

Tinkerbell'.

'Oh, it wasn't a dream!'

Sophie Barrett (13)
The Neale-Wade Community College, March

Best Friends

Sophie and I have been friends for ages, in fact we've been best friends for as long as I can remember.

Then it all went wrong, I didn't know what to do, I didn't know what to say to her. Whenever we were around each other - silence. Whenever we were near each other - silence. I didn't know what I'd done but when I saw her we ignored each other.

Maybe it was because I told her I was moving to Spain, but that wasn't my fault, I couldn't change my parents' minds. She didn't understand how upset I was when Mum and Dad told me we were moving! I was so upset that I locked myself in my bedroom and didn't come out for over a week, not even for chocolate and that's a first!

The downside to this was that, at the time, it was the holidays so it didn't matter if I stayed in my room as I wasn't going to miss school anyway!

Now back to the main idea of the story . . .

I was beginning to wonder whether we were ever going to be friends again, let alone best friends! Maybe she'd made a new best friend, even worse, what if she was now best friends with Stacey? Okay now I'm beginning to sound jealous. Well maybe I am jealous. Oh I don't know anymore. I just want to be normal again, like it was before.

What am I going to do? Everything is a disaster!

Laura Haslegrave (13)
The Neale-Wade Community College, March

My Wish . . .

'Don't you ever wonder, Victoria, what it would be like to be popular?' my friend asked me.

'Yeah, it would be great but there's no chance of that!' I said back to her.

'Yeah, I mean people say we're the geeks of the school!'

Then they came, the most popular kids, I mean, everyone knows them and all the boys fancy them.

'Oh my God! They're coming over here!' Jodie screeched. And they were!

Adele, Chloe, Toni, Jenny, Chantel, C-J and Becky came over . . . and walked straight past! I just wish sometimes that I was that popular.

The day dragged on as slow as ever and finally the bell rang. I was unfortunately last to get out as everyone trampled over me.

I finally got home and the day carried on, boring as ever.

'I bought a lottery ticket Victoria!' Mum said, shoving it in my face.

I tried to explain that there was no point but she still checked the numbers.

'Oh my *God!*' Mum shouted ecstatically.

'Mum, stop fooling around,' I joked.

'I'm not!' she said. 'We've *won,* I have all the numbers!'

I checked and she wasn't lying, I was also ecstatic!

The next day I told my friends and by the end of school, it had spread all over the school. I mean even the coolest girls in school wanted to hang around with me and talk to me.

My family and I now get to buy the latest gear and we go out all the time. People always hang around with me and for once I feel great. I was popular, happy and *rich!* Gradually my life got better but people accept me for being me and not for just being *rich.*

Victoria Roche (12)
The Neale-Wade Community College, March

A Day In The Life Of A Geek

Ever known what it feels like to walk in a classroom and everybody stares? When they don't have anything nice to say apart from, 'Freak! Loser! Geek!'?

I may look a bit different and I may not be as pretty as those popular girls, but that ain't a good enough reason to tease me!

Sometimes I think why can't I just be dead? Maybe my mum shouldn't have had me! I'm not fat or anything, it's just my face is a bit spotty and my hair isn't the best colour, it's ginger. I dye it a lot but after a while, it just goes away again.

I really do hate it when people say things about me. It makes me want to cry, but I don't cry, I think to myself, *I may not have much but I have tears and I'm not just going to give them away for you.*

My mum and dad are fairly rich so they give me quite a bit of money. That's when I used to have friends. They didn't want me, they only wanted my money.

School life is bad but only in certain subjects, because when we do group work, I'm always alone or the teacher makes me go with someone who you can tell really doesn't want to go with me.

I'm always the one sitting at the back of the classroom, all alone, hoping that home time will come quickly.

Home life is okay as I have loving parents, but it's lonely here too as I have no one to play with. Sometimes I sit in my room with a knife against my stomach with a little thing in my heart to my brain telling me to push. But then I think maybe I'll wake up tomorrow and life will be better. Maybe then I will be the popular girl! Maybe things will change.

Chloe Schunmann (13)
The Neale-Wade Community College, March

The Horror Test

It was a cold, pitch-black night and the old house was creaking from head to toe.

My name is Steve and I am doing a dare, well a test, to see if I have courage to join a gang.

It was getting on for eleven o'clock as I took yet another glimpse at the grandfather clock, I was waiting in the living room. It was a tall room, torn apart and covered in dust but the features that caught my eye were the portraits on the wall. They were horrid, one showed a family that looked as though they had been mutated into some monsters. Some people said that's what the happy family looked like after the massacre, others say it was just the family's freaky portrait - *bang!* There was a sudden noise from the next room, I became stiff.

Slowly I stumbled to my feet, scared and frightened of the sudden noise. I was going to check it out. Determinedly I strolled to the door, cautious of any noise or disturbance. I became frozen outside the door but forced myself to open it. I wish I hadn't. I screamed in horror and sprinted to the front door. 'Damn!' Locked. I sprinted back into the living room and slammed the door shut and locked it. I breathed a sigh of relief as I slowly turned round. I gasped, to my horror they were gone - the faces in the portraits were gone!

Dean Russell (14)
The Neale-Wade Community College, March

Living A Lie

My true identity is Eleanor Gibson. I look for men, marry them, then take all their money. Some would call me evil, I call myself a pure genius!

I have over a million pounds. I look for rich men. Loaded but vulnerable. I have been known under the names of Alicia White, Emily Reed and many more names. Nobody will ever find me because they're not as clever as I am! I never get too involved with people, in case of a sticky situation. I always leave six months between each man, so that I can lie low for a while. Life is great for me.

I don't do friends, friends always betray me. Life betrays me. I try to pretend I love my life but I don't, I'm so insecure. I hurt people for pleasure. People hurt me so I get revenge. I wine and dine in luxury, but I hate them!

My parents died when I was fourteen. I almost believe that if I die I would be wiped of all hatred. That's not true though.

My true identity is Eleanor Gibson. I look for men, marry them, then take all their money. Some call me evil, I call myself a pure genius.

Isabel Hurst (12)
The Neale-Wade Community College, March

The Beast's Conscience!

Along he crawls, down the alley, crawling, crawling, ready for his prey. Anyone, anything will do. Just for the taste of blood on his lips. He slithers along the floor, stopping occasionally, this time he hears some heels, clip-clapping, trip-trapping down the alley. Finally, the beast has found himself a feast!

The foolish young child, out all alone. Where are her friends? They should be with her. Oh why does he care, a meal. He's been so patient and now here is his chance. He waits until she comes striding by and -

Yes! He had his meal at last. The taste was as he imagined it. The sensation whizzing around his digestive system.

His conscience was starting to kick in. How young was this girl? Fourteen? Fifteen? She had her whole life ahead of her. Her parents wouldn't find out until it was too late. He had only knocked her out and bitten off her arm, maybe if he ran away she may live.

But there was another voice in my head, besides his conscience. It told him to carry on, told him not to care. But he was stuck, he didn't know what to do. Life was supposed to be easy as a beast. Creep around in the night-time, pounce on passers-by, eat them down to the bones, then leave them for someone else to discover. But it wasn't as simple as that, was it? He had found his conscience and had started to feel guilty.

Lorna Larham (12)
The Neale-Wade Community College, March

A Road To Death

The end of life as we know it has come, the armies of the Dark Lord are massing. But first I must tell you how this happened . . .

Many years ago the humans of Earth fought with the Dark Lord and managed to imprison him on the Earth.

Slowly, story turned to legend and legend turned to myths until many things were forgotten.

One day Alex was biking down a hill trying to break his speed record. He zoomed past hills with the wind in his face. The smell of spring was invigorating as we rode, past tree and flower. This in effect made him unconscious of the fact that he was about to hit a tree.

Smack! He fell and rolled at high speed into a small cave where he fell onto a large metal surface, he accidentally cut his hand on a rock, his blood fell onto the surface, a light emitted from it.

Alex ran as fast as he could but was unable to escape the blast from the cave which emitted light a hundred acres all around him. Out of the hole some ten foot tall being clothed completely in black arose.

Growing in his power, soon he will release his relentless armies and the world of evil will reign supreme.

Luke Deighton (12)
The Neale-Wade Community College, March

The Dummy

I opened the garage door as I trembled with fear. *Creeaakk!* That was the most terrifying noise I had ever heard. All I wanted to get was a little tub of paint. *Get a grip!* I thought to myself. *It's only a garage, I mean how scary can it be?* Understatement of the year I later found out.

I walked one step at a time as slowly as I could in case I woke the dead or anything. I mean, that couldn't really happen, could it? There it was, there was the little tub of lilac paint for my bedroom. But it was under a lot of old cobwebs and a lot of dust. *How much worse could this get?* I thought to myself. Also sitting there was a dummy and a shiny and very lifelike marble hand. A lot worse!

I walked over, my heart pumping so loud and quickly it made the room echo. I walked over to move the marble hand so I could get to the paint. I started to lift it up and realised everything was going fine, thankfully, and then suddenly *snap!* One of the fingers moved, was I imagining it or was it real? I didn't know just yet. All I knew was that it was certainly very creepy.

I was just then starting to think it really was my imagination . . . I tried to scream but nothing came out. The hand had jumped out of my hand and walked over to the dummy. The dummy had a hand missing. It was all starting to make sense, the hand belonged to the dummy and so I also realised that if the hand was alive then *(gulp)* so was the dummy!

I walked slowly back to the door of the garage so I could get out. Before I got there I heard a shuffling noise, then footsteps getting closer and closer. Suddenly I felt a cold draught. *Bang!* The garage door slammed shut. I walked over to the door, it was locked. I turned around . . . *aaarrrggghhh!*

Lauren Lakey (11)
The Neale Wade Community College, March

Myth of Ragnarock

An ordinary myth you think? Well ladies and gents of the audience, that is where you're wrong!

It is the year 19,653. Jack was on a plane over Iceland, but he was on no ordinary trip. He wanted the staff of Ragnarock, also known as Doomsday.

'Sir, the landing strip is ahead,' exclaimed the pilot.

The plane landed along the ice-covered landing strip.

Jack clambered out and looked around. 'There!' he pointed. 'That is Ragnarock Castle.' And he was correct.

Hovering over the mountain was the castle. 'How are we going to get up there Sir?'

'Don't worry.' He pulled a blaster out from his backpack. He shot the blaster at the castle. It blew up and the staff fell towards him.

Quickly, the pilot jumped and put the staff in the ground. Out came Vakama the ice lord. The massive creature picked him up and carried him to the volcano.

Jack realised that the pilot was going to summon Ragnarock instead of killing every bad person in the world. Running, Jack got to the volcano, but he was too late. Nokama the fire lord had been summoned.

The pilot said the words of Ragnarock, 'The ice lord will turn the ground to ice and the fire lord will set the sky ablaze.'

Jack threw the staff at the fire lord who melted it. 'If no one can use the staff for good, then no one will have it,' explained Jack.

Jonathon Bulbrook (11)
The Neale Wade Community College, March

A Day In The Life Of Tracey Pike

Tracey Pike may seem like a quiet girl but secretly she's not.

Every day is the same and cannot be changed. You see years ago she had a spell put on her and now it won't go.

It starts off by her waking up and eating her food. The same old cold porridge and maybe something new.

Then she goes on a secret mission and captures the baddies.

Later on, she might go to the park and be a spy. However, she does have lots of homework to do.

Then it comes to the end of the day and she's worn out. All she wants to do is go to sleep, although she can't.

Something inside her makes her feel ill and sick. So all she can do is watch the shining stars go by, until the next day, when it starts all over again!

Zara Head (12)
The Neale Wade Community College, March

Rescued! (An Extract)

It was a damp cold night in London. Everything was quiet, a bit too quiet. A rumour was going around that the world-dominating Germans were headed for England and starting their raid tonight. I wasn't sure if it was actually true, but even if it was, we were all prepared for it. The police had checked the siren over twelve times, at least! It was ringing in my head, it wouldn't stop. But to be honest, I wasn't really that bothered and neither was James. We weren't scared at all, why was it such a big deal? Could the Germans really beat us? I didn't think so, not with my dad in the air force, no way! He and his friend Henry always stayed longer hours after work to train extra hard. And sometimes at night I had dreams about my dad in his plane, flying skilfully around all the Germans, destroying every enemy plane. I wondered if we would win the war?

James and I were very different people. He loved everything and was good at it, but of course I wasn't. Anyway James and I loved playing and would play anything, anywhere. Places like dumps and rundown houses didn't seem scary when I was with James. We were on our way to probably my favourite location, the ruined houses on the corner. I didn't know that this hideout of ours would cause so much trouble.

It was a Tuesday morning when I left to play with James. We decided together that we should visit the old ruined building on the corner. We stayed all day, deep into the afternoon, playing the game of today, - 'tag'. We ran around the house like headless chickens. Dashing here and there without a care in the world. Knocking each other down, laughing loudly and genuinely playing a child's game, it was great. But then the Germans had to interrupt our fun, the siren went telling us that we would have to return home. We looked out of the door and saw a huge crowd of people dashing by. Instead of going outside and being knocked over, we decided to wait and to continue playing 'tag'.

As the crowd passed, James said to me, 'Look, shall we stay here and keep playing? This is probably just a test, no one will find us here and the Germans aren't gonna come, are they?'

Stupidly, I replied and said the worst thing I could have said on that night, 'I guess not!' But luckily I came to my senses and said, 'No!' I wanted to go back, but too late, things got ugly.

James got angry and started crying before pounding the house wall with a discarded iron bar which was lying amongst the stone. The wall crumbled and fell to the floor, collapsing all around us. James screamed and fell to the ground. The rubble was too strong for both of us as it continued to crush our feeble bodies. James scrambled, I heard a crack and then I felt it. Then I heard another struggle, James screamed.

'James, where are you? What's the matter?' I cried.

'It's okay Pete, I'm safe I'll go and get help, can you hear me, I'll go and get . . .'

'Get what James? Get what? James!' I heard footsteps running and dying away. I couldn't believe he would have just left me there. I wouldn't believe it. James was my best friend and I tried to think happy thoughts, but in the bottom of my stomach I knew that I was here with a broken leg and completely trapped. I lay, terrified, waiting . . .

William Piper (12)
The Neale Wade Community College, March

Dreams

The sun was glaring! Luke and James set off for the rundown, shabby stadium. James had just met Luke at school. Luke had dark green eyes as green as grass, and James was extremely small, he was a dwarf!

'Why are we going to this old place?' questioned James.

'Play footie!' answered Luke.

They were there in five minutes. They put the ball on the pitch. Suddenly, Luke grabbed James! James vaporised! Luke's skin, eyes, hair changed; he was James! Luke was brighter than James, although James had the only important thing Luke wanted - a loving family.

Luke had learned Egyptian spells to transform into James. James' soul was trapped in that stadium forever!

And here I am writing this childhood memory. Nobody will know my past and there is only one way to stop me . . .

Luke Barron (12)
The Neale Wade Community College, March

Hercules And Hydra

'Don't fear, I'm here!' shouted Hercules, jumping off the cliff and drawing his light sabre. In one smooth action, he struck the Hydra's head and it fell to the ground. Instantly three extra heads grew out of the bleeding stump that was once the neck of one. *How can I defeat this ugly brute!* pondered Hercules.

Fortunately for him he dropped his light sabre onto a pile of dry brush and twigs, causing a fire which would prevent the Hydra from growing more heads.

Using his new found advantage, Hercules attacked the Hydra with devastating effect. Heads flew and green blood sprayed everywhere. Very soon the Hydra was reduced to a quivering mass of green blood and muscle. Hercules was the hero!

James Beresford (12)
The Neale-Wade Community College, March

A Day In The Life Of A Footballer

I pull up at the training ground and push my door open of my brand new Honda Accord and go to the boot to get my boots, shin pads and bottle of water out. I make my way to the pitch and my manager says that I have a pay rise and I'm happy with myself because I'm moving to Real Madrid for ten million!

It is today that I move to Madrid. I am nervous - just in case I'm not good enough. When I arrive in Madrid, the wall of heat hits me. I don't know how I can play in this heat. All the reporters run towards me, they say, 'How do you feel about playing for Real Madrid?'

I say, 'Very happy because it's a dream come true!'

I drove to Real Madrid's training ground and the first player I see is Raul, the captain of Madrid.

I am training, and the manager comes to see me and says, 'Well done, you're a sub.'

I am happy because I got into the team as a sub.

The next two months are a blur but the greatest memory is scoring a goal against A C Milan in the Champions League.

Ashley Durance (14)
The Neale-Wade Community College, March

The Miracle Baby

The miracle baby had just arrived. Hilary Mclean was really surprised, it actually talked. Everyone thought we were insane, the midwife left in a state of shock. Nobody ever imagined a talking newborn baby.

When we left the newborn for half an hour she was already walking around reading the newspaper! Astonished, everyone stood back and gasped, stupefied. Nobody could make anything of it, a newborn walking and talking.

Every day seemed like five years. What seemed like an innocent little baby, soon became an intellectual computer programmer who then became a computer doctor, who then turned into the next Bill Gates.

But later that day people were getting worried. The baby (no longer) was growing ill. The baby now looked like a granny, old and frail with a stooped back. At the age of three years she was dying of old age. The family were worried and she was rushed to hospital!

While lying in the hospital bed, Granny asked to be reunited with her father. By the time he had arrived she had already passed away! The miracle no longer lived.

Zoey Ballard (14)
The Neale Wade Community College, March

A Day In The Life Of God

Hi, my name is God. I am a very busy person. My job is to help, save, control and change. I help people, save people, control the weather and change people's lives.

I don't get to sleep very much because I am God. I answer people's prayers. Some people have a lot to say. When I wake up in the morning I decide what the weather will be. (I think it should be sunny and dry today). Secondly, I answer people's prayers over breakfast. It is really hard but I can do it fast because I am God!

If the Devil creates any problems I get a red alert! I can also stop natural disasters from getting worse. Over 1,000 people die because of the Devil every day.

Because I can change lives people pray for better lives or more money and even to be the most famous, richest person in the world. It is really hard to not give them what they want. I can change some people's lives but some people are ignorant. They want to be me or be the best person in the world, it disgusts me!

I have had enough of this job. I think I will give it to someone else. Let me think . . . I know, how about Daniel Smith? He does everything he is told and he does not want anything in return. It is time for me to disappear forever. Goodbye and it has been nice talking to you.

Daniel Smith (14)
The Neale Wade Community College, March

A Day In The Life Of A Bird

A day in the life of a bird was so strange.

I woke up to find I had wings instead of arms. I stood up, flew to the window and flew through the sky so fast, the wind was in my face. I got back down on the ground and was looking for food - long, juicy worms. I searched for a few minutes then suddenly one popped its head out of the soil. So I quickly grabbed it and it was so nice since I'd had nothing to eat all day.

I tried to make a nest. It was hard at first but it got easier after a while. I finally finished and I got in to test it. The nest was so comfortable I felt like falling asleep but I knew there was lots more to do and see.

It was great being a bird till I saw a cat. I stopped for a second then turned round and flew as fast as I could. Finally, after a long time of flying fast I stopped. I was so relieved that I could finally rest my wings and take a long, deep breath.

I finally flew back to the nest and got myself comfortable and I began to sing. After a while I sang myself to sleep.

Becca Flattley (13)
The Neale-Wade Community College, March

A Day In The Life Of A Cat

I was going for a walk when I saw another animal. It looked really evil and I thought it was going to come after me.

I was very hungry and needed some milk, but there was nothing around me to eat or drink so I had to wait till I could have something. My legs were aching so I went to sleep and had a rest on the grass for a while. It was quite cold and windy. My long black fur kept blowing, nearly pulling me over when I got up.

Later on I went home and got some food and drink. Then I played with my ball, running around the house getting in trouble for nearly breaking things. I got chucked out of the house.

It was a really nice, warm day so I didn't do any running around. I just felt lazy and tired.

Hours later there were these other big, fat cats who were bigger than me. I was scared because they were coming towards me so I ran to find somewhere to hide, but they were following me. I think they were after me, I don't know why. They ran straight past me, that was lucky. There was a storm coming. I kept meaning to get back in the house.

It was almost night-time and I was lying, getting rest as I had had a horrible day thinking something was going to happen to me.

Rachel Symonds (14)
The Neale Wade Community College, March

A Day In The Life Of Me

Hi I'm Emma, I am an ordinary eleven-year-old. I live with my mum, Samantha and my brother Amwell, my Indian stepbrother. Me and Amwell always fight and argue about friends because when my friend Thomas comes round to help out with the homework, Amwell takes him away.

It all started one day when I came home from school and Mum was sitting at the breakfast bar with a fag in her mouth and a glass of vodka in her hands, as well as crying.

'It's going to be a long night,' I said in a hypo mood.

Mum was gasping for air as she was trying to say something to me. As she dried her tears, she said, 'Don't tell Amwell.' She ran upstairs as Amwell just walked through the door. Mum ran so fast a gust of wind blew a piece of paper from the breakfast bar onto the floor.

Amwell came in and asked, 'What's the matter with Mum?'

I picked up the paper and hid it in my pocket.

I said, 'Nothing, she's not well, just leave her alone.'

Amwell went upstairs, while I was at the bottom, making sure that he would go to his room and not see Mum. I grabbed the paper from my pocket and read it in surprise. It read:

'Dear Madam,

We are writing to you to set the date for you attending court. The date we would like for you to attend is 16th August 2004. Thank you.'

The magistrates' court. My heart sank. I was desperate to find out what the matter was.

It was one month till court . . .

Stacy Pearson (13)
The Neale-Wade Community College, March

Short Story

It was on a shiny, bright morning when the trees were swaying from side to side. The birds were out, singing away. I thought to myself, *absolutely nothing can go wrong.* Then, all of a sudden, I thought I heard a gunshot in the woods. I rushed to my hall to get my shotgun just in case someone or something attacked me.

I quickly rushed to the woods. There was no light in the woods so I had to take my pocket torch. When I had hold of the torch, *wham!* Someone or something didn't want me there. I thought I wasn't going to survive.

My instinct was to run so I got up, holding my head. I ran so fast nothing could catch up with me. I got into my garden and there was blood all over my garden and when I got near my door, there was a body on my steps. I froze in fear. I thought to myself, *that could have been me lying on the steps, dead.* I turned the body over. 'Oh no!' I shouted, it was my twin brother. He had been killed for something I had done.

I heard a sound behind me. I looked round, there was no one there. I listened again. *Click, click,* it sounded like a gun getting ready to fire.

I quickly ran out of the garden. *Bang!* Thankfully it missed me and hit the road.

I kept on running but still could hear breathing behind me . . .

Peter James (13)
The Neale-Wade Community College, March

Scottish Sea Monster

Is it true or not?

No one knows what Simon McBeth saw that night in the Scottish lake.

A sea monster appeared out of dark waters. In the moonlight it looked like a sea serpent but it smelt like a rotten fish.

As it came out of the water, it had two arms and four legs and scales like a dragon. While it came out of the water it was breathing ice-breath and froze the ground, then went back into the water.

Simon McBeth ran back to the village but while he was running back, the sea serpent swam back to shore, climbed out and killed some sheep and ate them.

The village people did not believe him at all.

Richard Jarrett (15)
The Parkside School (MLD), Norwich

Biggest Super Bank Robbery

On Friday 13th, Billy escaped from jail. He stole a car, he got a man and went to the gun shop and stole some guns. He got in the stolen car and went in the bank. He got out his sniper rifle and shot the police car's tyres. It crashed into a petrol tanker and thousands of litres of petrol poured out, but the policeman escaped before it blew up.

Billy got the man to go into the bank. The man blew up the bank. The police, two people and William Page saw the man who shot the tyres of the police car and described him to the police.

Billy shot the policeman through the neck. His name was Shane. Billy stole a helicopter and shot the police van which crashed into the school bus.

One of the kids broke his arm. The police got a laser bomb but it missed the helicopter.

Somebody moaned to Jason, 'Did you put any petrol in the helicopter?'

'No I didn't!'

Billy crashed into the sea. The police found the helicopter but his body wasn't there.

It is a mystery!

William Page (14)
The Parkside School (MLD), Norwich

Norwich In Darkness

Electricity fault at power station leaves Norwich in darkness.

The manager of the power station is investigating how the problem started. He said that he hoped to find what started it by the end of the week.

One of our best reporters interviewed a man called Ben, who was working at the power station when the power went out. He said that he went to get a cup of coffee when the lights flickered. Ben said that he went to get his lunch which he'd left in the dining room. He had just finished his lunch when the lights started to flicker for five minutes and then they went out. Ben went to the generator but it was not working. He didn't know what to do, so he rang the manager.

If you want any more information, visit our website, www.edp.com.uk.

Damian Burden (15)
The Parkside School (MLD), Norwich

Biggest Pub Fight Ever

Local Norwich pub was under attack with petrol bombs and fireworks.

A local pub in Norwich was badly damaged from the world's biggest fight at King's Pub in King's Street yesterday, after closing time at 1am. 8 people have been pronounced dead after fireworks and petrol bombs were thrown inside the pub. 4 people are badly injured. 2 men in masks are wanted for the petrol bombings. They are described as 8 feet 6 inches tall, tattoos on their hands, black masks, black jumpers and black trousers. The other men were described as 18 or 19 years old, covered in tattoos and have six-packs.

Mr Dick Boots, an eyewitness who was nearby, said, 'It was a horrible sight but there were a lot more people getting into the fight and 2 men banged past me wearing black with masks on and started to throw petrol bombs. I phoned the police and started to run to break the fight up. As the police arrived, I went under a lamp post to see if I was bleeding but I was not'.

Mr William Time, a night-time lorry driver for MBM was driving by when he saw a firework being thrown into the building. He said, 'I thought there was a party in the pub but when I went past the pub entrance I saw a hell of a fight and got out of my lorry to break it up. I saw 2 men in masks with petrol bombs so I moved my lorry in case it went up in flames. Soon I saw about 2 or 3 police helicopters flying around so I went away before I got arrested . . .'

At about 2.16am, 11 arrests were made and police found drugs - heroin and cocaine.

For the next 5 weeks, the King's Pub and King's Street will be closed for investigations to find out what started the big fight.

Anyone with information about the fight or the men with the petrol bombs please call Norwich police or Crimestoppers.

Mark Chatten (15)
The Parkside School (MLD), Norwich

Eastending

Rumour is that EastEnders is ending after Coronation Street's victory at the Soap Awards. They've won 10 years in a row.

EastEnders hasn't won an award for best soap for 10 years and is going to be axed at the end of the year. The plan is Albert Square is going to be blown up in a dramatic way. Who will survive?

At one time EastEnders was the best soap around and people will miss it. It's going the way of Crossroads, Brookside, Night And Day, Family Affairs, Emmerdale and Hollyoaks.

We spoke to Letitia Dean aka Sharon Watts, she has been in Walford for the best part of her life and she said she will miss the cast and miss working on the square.

We also spoke to Mrs Howard of Parkside School in Norwich who said, 'I've been a fan of EastEnders since the beginning, it's my favourite soap and I don't know what I'll do when it finishes. I won't bother watching Coronation Street, it's boring'.

At the moment there are only 2 British soaps - Coronation Street and EastEnders and 2 Australian soaps - Home and Away and Neighbours.

Over the past 10 years EastEnders has lost millions of viewers all around the world so it does deserve to be axed.

What do you think about this? Vote now on www.bbc.co.uk/East-Enders or vote in today's Sun.

Send all votes to The Sun, PO Box London 2427.

Paul Jackson (15)
The Parkside School (MLD), Norwich

Fear

John Chessington was a fine lad who excelled at school and sports. The only problem was his personality. You see, John got pleasure from torturing his twin, Nick, who not only had a heart defect, but also severe arachnophobia. Nick couldn't stand spiders. He hated all eight of their hairy legs, and he hated their many eyes. If there was one in a room he would discreetly leave.

On their twelfth birthday they were at the zoo when a large man ran into Nick, sending him flying forward onto the glass. A spider was sitting on the other side. Nick's eyes widened and he screamed, running away and scratching his face. John chuckled quietly and went to buy something at the zoo's shop.

What he bought, John would never tell.

As the years rolled by, Nick and John became the best of friends. On their birthday, John still liked to buy something from the zoo shop.

One year the boys were at home to celebrate. John said they were opening presents in their bedrooms. As Nick followed him up, his heart was racing with excitement. John led Nick into a room as black as night, then switched on the lights to reveal . . . tarantulas!

They were everywhere, swarming over the walls, ceiling and floor. They crawled up his legs and fell into his hair. The last thing he saw before his fatal heart attack was John in hysterical laughter.

Robin Culshaw (11)
The Perse School, Cambridge